A City; a Secret; a Broken Shoe

by Barry A. Enns

Copyright © 2012 by Barry A. Enns
First Edition – December 2012

ISBN
978-1-4602-0828-1 (Hardcover)
978-1-4602-0826-7 (Paperback)
978-1-4602-0827-4 (eBook)

The author would like to thank all those who encouraged him with their love and support. You know who you are.

All rights reserved.

Edited by: Carol A. Pelton

Illustration by: Callum McKendry

No part of this publication may be reproduced in any form, or by any means, electronic or mechanical, including photocopying, recording, or any information browsing, storage, or retrieval system, without permission in writing from the publisher.

Produced by:

FriesenPress
Suite 300 – 852 Fort Street
Victoria, BC, Canada V8W 1H8

www.friesenpress.com

Distributed to the trade by The Ingram Book Company

CHAPTER ONE

In three weeks I would be turning sixteen years old. Twenty minutes ago, I could think of little else. Sixteen meant a driver's licence. A driver's licence meant I could take the car I had been fixing up for the past year on its first test drive. I put blood, sweat and tears not to mention hundreds of hours of my time and money into that car and now it was ready to go. The car meant my freedom. There was a whole wide world out there and soon I would be exploring it. Things were going to be great. Unfortunately, that was twenty minutes ago.

Right now, I found myself locked up in the back seat of a police car. Twenty minutes ago, I was on my way home from the auto wrecker where I spent most of my spare time. I turned onto my block and noticed flames coming from the roof of a neighbourhood home. Running to the first door I saw with a light on, I began ringing the bell and pounding on the door. When I heard someone moving around inside, I pounded even harder. As I went around the corner of the house to look in the window, I noticed someone running down the back alley. I wasn't sure but the person looked a lot like the owner of the house that was on fire. He was wearing a baseball cap and had the hood of his sweater pulled up over his head. I heard the door open behind me, so I turned and asked the elderly gentleman who lived there to call the fire department although I knew it was a waste of time. He could see the flames as easily as I. He turned to run back inside to use the phone, but first he told me to grab the garden hose that was coiled up against the far side of his house and turn it on.

I watched as first the fire department and then the police showed up, lights flashing and sirens screaming. I alternated directing the feeble stream of water from the garden hose between the old guy's garage and the roof of his house. There were a few sparks flying around so I did what I could to put them out before they did any more damage.

I watched in fascination as the men from the fire department strung out hoses, pulled out ladders and hooked up their hoses to the fire hydrants. The speed and grace they displayed could only come from long hours of practice. It was a totally different story watching the police. Two squad cars arrived simultaneously. One of them drove up onto a neighbour's yard leaving huge skid marks in his well-manicured lawn and the other parked on the street between the fire truck and fire hydrant. The officer jumped out. Only after a fire fighter threatened to break out the windows of his car did he get back in and move it. I recognized both officers, but, I didn't know their names. They were community police officers and I had seen them around in the course of their duties: at accident scenes, handing out traffic tickets and on occasion, putting on presentations at the school. I watched them leaning against the fire truck with take-out coffee cups in one hand and their radio microphones in the other.

The larger of the two kept looking in my direction, but I thought nothing of it until he said something to his partner and headed towards me. He approached me with a hand on the butt of his gun. The thought of leaving never crossed my mind. Why would I? On the other hand, I was a teenager. I did think about spraying him with the water hose. It was a only a passing thought but the officer must have seen something in my eyes because he stood just out of reach of the stream of water and told me to shut it off. I was going to tell him to shove it. The owner of the house walked up behind me and after thanking me, took the hose.

People were lined up all along the block. The news must have spread to nearby neighbourhoods because there were far more onlookers than residents on our street. Every one of them watched as the officer grabbed me by the arm and shirt collar and half-dragged me to the police car parked on the lawn. He ignored my many protests and refused to answer when I asked him what I did wrong. I tried to tell him about the man I saw running away. He just grinned, told me to shut up and none too gently, threw me in the back seat of his car. I was only partially inside when he slammed the door closed catching my elbow. It hurt. I was sure that I would be sporting a bruise for the next few days.

The pleasant thoughts of a few minutes ago were a distant memory. In their place were confusion, fear and yes, a little bit of anger. Well, maybe a whole lot of anger. With nothing to do but watch and wait, I turned in the seat to see what was happening around me. There was a lot to see. More fire trucks and police cars were arriving by the minute. The flames were growing bigger, despite the best efforts of the fire fighters. The house that was on fire was a lost cause, so they opted to protect the one's closest to it. Under different circumstances, I might have enjoyed the scene. The sounds of the crowd, sirens, and roaring flames were mesmerizing. Throw in the bright orange of the flames, the red, white and blues of the flashing lights and the early evening darkness; you were left with a scene that even Picasso might have appreciated.

I watched the group of policemen that included Officer Dan Carruthers. Dan Carruthers was the name of the bad-breathed, overweight red-neck that locked me in the car. I read his name off the tag that was pinned to his shirt pocket. It was a name I would not soon forget. They didn't appear to be doing much. There was a lot of talking and occasionally one or the other of the officers would walk towards the crowd that surrounded the scene and push them back. I watched as the elderly gentleman whose door I knocked on walked toward them. It was obvious when they all turned toward me that I was the subject of their conversation. There was much gesturing and pointing, but eventually, he turned from the group and walked towards me. Between the crowd noise and closed window it was hard to hear him, but I am sure he said something to the effect that things would work out for me. I waved half-heartedly as he returned to his own yard and the garden hose that still sprayed water.

For the first time, I took a good look at the crowd that was growing by the minute. I knew a lot of them. They were after all my neighbours and had been ever since I was born. I noticed that quite a few were pleased to see me in this awkward predicament. My name is Malcolm Webb. The Webb's have lived in the town of Parkfield for three generations. Last Thanksgiving, twenty-three people showed up at my grandparent's for our annual family get-together. All of them lived in or around Parkfield. That number usually exceeds thirty, but two cousins and an uncle were in jail; an aunt, an uncle and a great-uncle were on the run from the police; and two cousins were afraid to show their faces.

The Webb's are, indeed, well-known. We are not known for our generosity, kindness, or community spirit. Our name is more often associated with petty theft, bounced cheques and bad tempers. Not all of us are convicted criminals. Some, like my mother, four cousins that I know of, and me have yet to commit a crime. Many others, like my father have clean records, only because they have not yet been caught. Even those with enough ambition to open their own businesses are more likely to invest in corner stores and towing companies, instead of, dry cleaners and movie theatres. It is hard to sell bootleg clothes and movies from a dry cleaners and impossible to operate a chop shop from a movie theatre.

Making friends has always been one of my biggest challenges. I am painfully shy and several pounds overweight. I wear thick glasses and when I get excited I develop an embarrassing stutter. It's hard to be outgoing and I am very self-conscious. How could I not be surprised by the crowd's apparent dislike? Even a couple family members were standing out front laughing and pointing at me.

Parkfield was a small city. It was big enough to attract yuppies to staff the office buildings that were sprouting up all over downtown, yet small enough to make the red-necks that populated the outlying areas feel right at home. It was small enough for its residents to believe that their children were safe walking to and from school, yet big enough to make crime profitable. Parkfield was home to a large tire manufacturer, a medium sized pharmaceutical company and a small college. It took pride in the fact that its hospital was the newest and most up-to-date in the region. In reality, Parkfield was indistinguishable from hundreds of other cities of the same size.

A look at my watch told me that two and a half hours had passed since I was thrown into the back of the police cruiser. In that two and half hours, no one, not even, Dan Carruthers had checked on my well-being. Maybe it is rude of me to refer to him as Dan rather than Officer but under these circumstances, I just didn't care. I wasn't quite desperate, but it wouldn't be long before I needed to use the restroom. Twice I had beckoned to Dan, and twice he ignored me and walked right past the car window. The flames were under control and many of the vehicles with their flashing lights were gone. The street lights and the nearby houses were completely dark so the electric company must have turned off the power as a precaution. The remaining firefighters were rolling up hoses when someone finally opened the door to the police car. The officer, who climbed into the front passenger seat, was much younger than Dan. I tried to read his name tag, but the interior light went out when he closed the door so I was not able to make it out. He turned in his seat to make it easier to talk to me. Under different circumstances, I might have appreciated his friendliness. However, right now, I was mad and I needed to use a washroom. He started by introducing himself, and telling me to call him Joe Grosjean. He spent the next several minutes trying to apologize for Dan's actions. As he was speaking, I noticed Dan heading in our direction, walking as fast as his bulk allowed. I watched as Dan was intercepted by two of the other officers. One of them put a hand on Dan's shoulder and the other stepped in front of him, cutting him off. Joe watched the scene unfolding before us and when Dan was finally led away, he told me that I was owed an explanation.

It was out of my sight, but supposedly a conversation that included a number of police officers took place. It was during this conversation that Dan explained to the others his reasons for grabbing me out of the neighbour's yard.

It seems that Dan recognized me the same way I recognized him. I was a resident in his beat. As we all know, a good police officer notices everything. I was, after all, a Webb. When Dan saw me standing in the yard next door to the fire, the first thing that came to his mind was the Webb name. Then he remembered a course that he was taking at the local college to ensure that he received an upcoming promotion. The course wasn't really necessary, he assured the others. It was obvious that he was the most qualified with the most seniority, but his wife had convinced him that taking courses in psychology and profiling would look good on his resume.

Anyway, Dan's psychology class that afternoon was on arson and arsonists. Dan remembered the instructor stressing that many arsonists will join the crowds that inevitably form around the flames. "Something about a compulsion to watch the havoc they have wreaked!" said Dan. As Dan drove up, I stood watching the fire. That alone might have convicted me, but adding in the Webb name, in his mind made it a no-brainer.

One of Dan's colleagues pointed out to him that hundreds of people were standing in the street watching the flames, including another Webb or two. According to Joe, it was a good argument, but Dan had the look of someone who had made his decision and was going to stick with it. Worse for me was that some of the other officers agreed with him.

Dan had plans for me that didn't include me sleeping in my own bed that night. Even the officers who agreed that I was guilty told Dan that it was a mistake to arrest me. "Gather some more evidence," they told him.

Dan was adamant that I be taken downtown until his cell phone rang. Joe, standing to one side had called the Supervisor who was on duty that night. He gave the Supervisor a brief overview and passed the phone to the nearest policeman who confirmed Joe's story. The Supervisor then called Dan and told him to let me go. Dan wasn't happy. Even in the darkness, I could see him staring in my direction.

No one, especially Dan, wanted to face me in the car. Joe, the newest member on the force, had the seniority clause invoked by the others at the scene forcing him to talk to me. In the end, I was glad the chore fell on Joe's shoulders.

I told Joe the same story I had told Dan. He was sceptical. Unlike Dan, he listened when I told him about the man I noticed running away just after the fire started. When I finally finished, Joe opened his door, jumped out of the front seat, and opened the door that separated me from my freedom. I wish I could describe the feeling of relief I felt. The right words still elude me. I now knew that a decision I made when I was about eleven years old was the right one. One of my cousins had asked me to help him steal a couple of chocolate bars from a grocery store. Telling him he was crazy, I ran for the door.

At that moment, like now, I could not understand why anyone would willingly risk their freedom for a few ill-gotten gains.

Before I climbed out, Joe offered me his card. He told me that for all he knew I was a no-account scoundrel just as Dan said. "Today, I will give you the benefit of the doubt. Please call me if I can help you with anything." he said. His last words were a warning. "Watch yourself. Dan will try to catch you doing something wrong. He may even set a trap."

I was free at last. By now, I really needed that washroom. The trees in the backyard beckoned. However, Joe's warning was still fresh in my mind. Despite, my discomfort, I opted to head for home. I walked by the group of police officers that included Carruthers. I didn't say a word, held my head high and matched his steely stare with one of my own. It was just my luck that the crowds that were present for my humiliation were nowhere to be seen at my moment of jubilation.

CHAPTER TWO

It was almost midnight by the time I arrived home. I understand that in a normal household, parents worry when their fifteen-year old isn't home at midnight on a school night. However, my home life is not normal. Not for a second did I expect to see someone waiting for me, but it still would have been nice to have a sympathetic ear present. The power to the neighbourhood had come back on as I was walking home. It caught me with my pants down, well my zipper anyway – I was taking advantage of the darkness and a huge oak tree to relieve myself. My home was one of the few on the block that still remained in darkness, so I knew that no one was home. There would be no shoulder to cry on tonight.

My mother left about ten years ago. She decided that making a better man out of my father was a job for someone else. I lived with her for a few years after she left. Once I became a teenager, I asked if I could move in with my father. She was reluctant, but I managed to convince her that I would not be influenced by my father's many bad habits. I used the old argument; "all young men need a strong male presence" to finally win her over. Six months later, she moved fifteen hundred miles to be with a man she had met on the internet. I haven't seen her since. We keep in touch by weekly phone calls.

The strong male presence proved to be a pipe dream. Instead of being present, my father spent most of his nights with one of his many girlfriends, or if not at a girlfriend's, he was out drinking with one of his buddies. Once I learned to look after myself, the arrangement worked out well. It pleased me to be able to look after myself. I could walk into a clean house and be proud of my work. I could sit down to enjoy a nutritious meal and be proud of my cooking.

It was great to be independent, but sometimes, even when you were almost sixteen you weren't too old to need a shoulder, maybe not to cry on, but at least to lean on. This was one of those times. I did what I always do when I am hurting, sad or depressed. I do the same thing when I am happy. I went to the garage to look at my 1977 Monte Carlo.

I turned on the light, but I really didn't need to. I knew the car like the back of my hand, better if possible. I found the car shortly after moving in with my father. He and I had been visiting the auto wrecker's that was partially-owned by my uncle, who had been recently released from jail. His latest stay in the penitentiary had been a short one. With luck, his latest attempt at freedom would last much longer. My father wanted to talk with him and I was invited along. The two men shooed me out of the office while they chatted so I wandered around looking at the vast collection of used cars and parts that covered almost every inch of the premises. While I waited, I noticed a car being towed into the compound. The tow truck driver parked in front of the office and walked inside to talk to the dispatcher. I went outside to look at the car.

It was the same Monte Carlo that I was looking at now. However, the windows were all broken, tires were flat and the paint was scratched. The antenna was broken, windshield wipers torn off and the landau roof had been sliced with a knife. The gas cap was missing and sugar or something could be seen on the rim of the filler spout. The car had been vandalized. By the looks of the car, the person who had done the vandalizing was both extremely angry and determined to do as much damage as possible.

The car was a mess. Closer examination showed that the fenders were in excellent shape. I took a peek underneath. Even to my untrained eyes, I could see that there was very little rust on the frame. The suspension and brakes appeared to be in decent shape as well. I found its unique appearance appealing. Its long hood and short trunk made it look as though it was built for speed not comfort. The car may have appeared unique, but many of its parts were not. The motor, transmission, wipers, headlights and many other pieces were ordinary Chevrolet parts that could be found almost anywhere. An idea was quickly taking shape in my mind.

I returned to the office and asked the tow truck driver about the car. He told me that it had just been picked up from the residence of its owner. The driver enjoyed telling the story and his enthusiasm ensured that he had the undivided attention of everyone in the shop, including my father and his brother who had returned to the front of the office.

Apparently, the Monte Carlo took the brunt of punishment when the owner's girlfriend found him naked in the back seat of the car with the girlfriend's sister. The owner was lucky that it was just his car. The sister, who was naked in the back seat with him, did not know that he was also seeing her sibling, who was now bashing in the windows. The owner found himself running down the street naked as the day he was born with two screaming sisters hot on his tail.

The owner returned to his car an hour later wearing a greasy pair of overalls given to him by a sympathetic passer-by. The car was trashed. His jeans and leather jacket were in shreds, his sneaker was sticking out of the exhaust pipe and his shirt was stuffed into the gas tank. The shirt had been lit on fire and was still smouldering when its owner carefully pulled it out in an effort, not to save the car which to him was already a total wreck, but to save the neighbourhood from what could have been a massive explosion.

A few weeks passed with much negotiating taking place, albeit from a distance between the owner and the sisters. Our friend, who owned the now-destroyed Monte Carlo was a quick learner and knew enough to stay away from the angry sisters. In the end, the sisters offered to pay a few hundred dollars to avoid a criminal record and to have the car hauled away to the wrecking yard.

I spent the next hour making a deal with my uncle, the co-owner and the manager. The car was cheap. I bought it for a hundred dollars, which was about the amount the wrecker would receive if they sold it for scrap steel. In order to transport the car to my place, I also had to pay five hundred dollars to buy an old trailer. I agreed to work for my uncle after school and weekends in order to pay off my debt and to earn the money I would need to restore the Monte Carlo. We hitched the trailer to my father's old pick-up, loaded up the Monte Carlo and headed home.

The very next day, I appeared at the wrecking yard prepared to go to work. It wasn't totally new to me. I was taking shop in high school. In some ways what I learned in shop helped with my work in the wrecking yard and my work at the wrecking yard most certainly helped me in shop. I enjoyed the work.

I had the yard pretty much to myself, except for a couple of mangy old dogs. The dogs resented me at first, but unlike most of the people I met, they grew to accept me. After a few weeks, they actually seemed to appreciate my company. My job was to catalogue and diagram the location of the various cars that were being stripped for parts. For years, the cars had been simply dumped in the first available space and forgotten. To the surprise of the owners, after several months, I managed to come up with a complete inventory list. Using my list, they began advertising parts for sale. I soon had a new job. Each day when I arrived, I was given a list of parts to locate. At first, someone came with me to remove the parts, but after a while I was given my own tools and allowed to remove the parts myself. I must have been pretty good at it because a lot of the regular customers waited until they knew I would be working and asked for me by name. The tips I received were frequent and generous. Within three months, the trailer and Monte Carlo were paid for and I had a substantial nest egg to buy parts.

I didn't expend all my energy for the benefit of the wrecker's owners. I also made a list of my own. I knew where to find all the parts that I was going to need for my own project. The parts I selected for myself were the best available.

The garage at home was too small to work on the Monte Carlo, so it usually sat in the back yard. I put up a string of lights in order to work on it late at night as that was the only time I was free. Except for the occasional Sunday, most of my daylight hours were spent either in school, or at the wrecking yard.

I didn't mind the late hours in the least. As trite as this may sound, it was indeed a labour of love. I fashioned a tarp to cover the car to protect it from the elements. I started by cleaning up the broken glass and stripping off the broken exterior parts.

Now the paint gleamed and well it should. I spent two months sanding it down to bare metal and paid hundreds of dollars to a local body shop to apply three coats of deep burgundy paint.

The chrome shone in the meagre light that reached it from the driveway. I was proud of the chrome. I had removed it piece by piece and polished it myself in shop class using equipment provided by the school. The hours turned to weeks, the weeks to months and now almost three years later it was ready to drive. First things first, I needed a license. I couldn't resist opening the door and turning on the ignition. The car immediately came to life. You could say it purred like a kitten but when I touched the gas pedal, the throaty roar that issued from its tailpipe indicated that this kitten would be right at home in the jungle. When the neighbour's light came on, I reluctantly turned the car off.

A neighbour started to complain the very first day I came home with the car. If I was using a hammer, he complained about the noise. If I was using a welder or torch, he complained about the sparks. He complained about the smell of oil and gas. He complained about the discarded old parts that I removed from the car even though I hauled them away the morning after they were removed.

The neighbour started the rumour that I was a thief the day I brought home the first tire. People were all too willing to believe him. Remember, I am a Webb. Webb's don't work so how could I afford the parts that I carried home on a daily basis. They assumed that I stole them. A number of times, I could see patrol cars parked on the street while I worked on the car. Twice I was stopped as I rode my bike down the street. Both times the officer asked to see the receipt for the parts that I was carrying in plain view. Maybe the Webb's weren't the most honest of people, but not a one of us would be stupid enough to ride a bike down the street with stolen car parts in our knapsack. I tried to be nice to the neighbours by raking their leaves, changing their flats and cleaning their gutters. Instead of thanking me, they picked up the phone and spread more lies. I don't know where they think I found the time to steal. Between school, the auto wrecker's and the Monte Carlo I was kept busy. Stealing was the last thing on my mind.

I closed and locked the garage door and headed for the house. It was now two a.m. and my father had yet to come home. I doubted if he would so I poured myself a glass of water from the fridge, turned off the lights and went to my bedroom. I undressed and crawled under the covers. I was tired, but sleep was elusive. I was haunted by thoughts of Officer Dan and the man I saw running away. Was he also lying awake somewhere on the other side of town?

I thought I knew who the running man was, but I was unwilling to swear to it. I was standing in light and looking into darkness as he ran by. The runner was in darkness and looking at me standing in the light. Maybe he didn't know my name, but I am sure he was able to see my face well enough to recognize it again. I was worried that the runner might consider me a threat and do me harm, but I was a whole lot more worried about the police.

Before I knew it, the sun had risen and the birds were singing cheerfully, eager to begin a new day. Their cheerfulness, though pleasant to hear, did little to brighten my outlook.

CHAPTER THREE

I finally marshalled enough energy to crawl out of bed. While I waited for my toast to pop, I put together a lunch that consisted of an apple and a ham and cheese sandwich. After a glass of juice and some toast and jam I was off to school. I suspected that I was in for a rough day, but nothing could have prepared me for the onslaught that I actually faced.

I walked the school hallway and the voices didn't stop. "Hey Webb, I heard you were in jail."

"Malcolm! Is it true you are an arsonist?"

"I heard you were caught with drugs last night."

"Were you crying in Dan's cop car?"

"Hey Webb, go back to jail where you belong!"

"Hide your matches. We have an arsonist among us."

It went on all morning. In the halls, in the classrooms and especially in the washroom, they refused to let it go. I tried to explain what happened but no one listened. My skin had grown quite thick over the years and it grew even thicker that day. I refused to let them get to me. I walked with my back straight and my head held high.

At noon, I grabbed the sandwich from my locker and headed for a side door that led to an area of the school grounds that was seldom used. I opened the door and the first thing I saw were two girls surrounded by a group of boys. I recognized the tall skinny girl at the center of the melee. Her name was Laura and we attended the same Geography and Science classes. The shorter girl was doing most of the shouting and jumping around. She appeared to be younger than Laura, but right now she was giving her tormentors almost all they could handle. I knew a couple of the boys to be high school seniors and a couple of the others were well-known athletes.

I watched for about twenty seconds, long enough to realize that the boys had stolen a bag of cookies from Laura and were now pushing and teasing her mercilessly. One of them reached for a knife that hung on his belt and threatened to cut off her pony tail. Something snapped inside me and disregarding the knife, I made a beeline for the crowd. I pushed everyone aside until I reached the boy holding the cookies that were now little more than a bag of crumbs. I closed my fist and swung for his stomach. The day's frustrations were manifested in that blow. While the recipient of my fist was gasping and retching, his friends were too stunned to react. The kid with the knife was so surprised that he dropped it. I grabbed Laura with one hand and her young friend with the other and headed around the corner.

I spent the rest of the lunch hour with the girls. We made sure that we were always within sight of a supervisor, in case the boys decided to seek revenge. Tracy, the shorter girl with glasses, was Laura's cousin. Despite the circumstances, I had to laugh at her antics. She was still spitting mad and some of her suggestions for payback were almost diabolical. Boiling water; tar and feathers; vises and dull spoons were all mentioned. To my amazement, she pulled the knife out from under her sweater. When she had picked it up, I had no idea.

For the most part Laura remained quiet. I thought some color was returning to her face, but it was hard to tell. Laura's complexion was fair at the best of times. Her hair was long and black and I remembered that a number of our classmates referred to her as Morticia from the Addams family. The hour passed quickly and I headed off to class with a chorus of Thank Yous echoing in my ear. It was a new feeling for me and I must say that I did enjoy it.

Once I was back inside the school, the talk began again. News of my encounter must have spread because now I was receiving almost as many threats as taunts. It wasn't all bad. Now that my fellow students knew that I could fight back, they made it a point to head in the opposite direction instead of laughing and gesturing when I faced them with their accusations. The final class of the day was Geography. I sat in my usual seat at the back of the class and watched as Laura walked into the room. She headed straight for the desk beside me that until now sat vacant. I met her shy smile with one of my own and together we stared down anyone with the audacity to snicker or point in our direction.

You have to understand that having a smiling girl sitting next to me was something that happened a lot in my dreams, but infrequently in real life. During the long lonely hours working on the car, I thought of the girls in my classes often. I knew all of their names and they took turns cheering me on during my heroic exploits. Arguments, over who was next to take my arm as we strolled down red carpets, weren't unheard of. Imagination is a wonderful thing.

Laura was in my thoughts more than most. Maybe there were prettier girls in the class, but I doubt it. She always struck me as being shy - something we had in common. What attracted me most was the fact that she didn't appear to have a boyfriend. Maybe she was available, a good omen in my books. According to the hallway gossip, most of our classmates were already paired off and out of my reach. Now we found ourselves sitting next to each other in class. Staring down our classmates wasn't a problem, but looking at each other was. We spent the entire class trying to steal glances at one another. When caught, our beet-red faces quickly turned to our open text books.

When class ended, we gathered our books and headed for the door. Neither of us said a word as I walked her to her locker. Tracy was waiting when we got there. She accepted my presence without comment. Laura dropped off her books, grabbed her jacket and after a short detour to my locker, the three of us made our way outdoors. Laura and I didn't have to talk much when Tracy was around. She talked enough for four people. She told us about her afternoon, the good and the bad. She told us what she planned to watch on television that entire week. She talked about her favourite singer, that she was having meatloaf for supper and we even heard about her dentist's purported affair. Before I knew what was happening, Tracy had learned where I lived and made plans for the three of us to walk to school together the following day. I was going to have to run to get to work in time, but I was disappointed just the same when we reached their street. I was sorry to have to leave them. If my heart fluttered when Laura said thank you to me earlier in the day, it positively threatened to leap out of my chest when she touched my arm and I swear, batted her eye lashes at me as we parted ways.

I ran the rest of the way to work. My heart was racing and the promise of a new-found love gave wings to my arms and legs. Wait a minute. I can't tell a lie. I hurried to work. Let's get real. I was a little overweight and incapable of running more than a block or two. All the same, I was out of breath when I arrived at the auto wrecker's. I entered the office to get my instructions. A number of people were standing around talking. From the number of coffee cups and cigarette butts that littered the area, they must have been talking for a while.

As I neared them, my uncle shouted out, "Hey Malcolm, did you hear about Tom Crawford?"

Tom Crawford was the man who owned the house that had burned last night. The same man I was sure I saw running from the fire. "Yeah, his house burned down. I was there," I said.

"No, not that, I know you were there. I hear the cops even tried to arrest you for it. That's a tough break. If you need a lawyer, I know a couple of good ones," he said. The others laughed with him. I wasn't offended by their laughter. Unlike the kids at school, these men were sympathetic to my plight. They had all suffered the same indignities, whether they deserved it or not, I wasn't about to judge.

Before my uncle could continue, one of the others said, "They found Tom's body in the wreckage this morning. It's been on the news all day."

Thoughts of Laura and her delicate touch were erased from my racing mind. They were replaced by images of running men and dead bodies. Tom Crawford's face appeared on both. My mind readily accepted the image of Tom Crawford running. A dead Tom Crawford was a different story. No matter how hard I tried, I could not accept it.

As quickly as the images of Tom appeared, they were replaced by darker thoughts. If someone died in the fire, was I the only suspect? Would Dan Carruthers or Joe Grosjean be waiting for me when I went home? I questioned the entire group, but learned little about the direction the investigation was taking.

This crowd was more than willing to talk about Tom Crawford, however. It was apparent that most of them knew him, by reputation, if not personally. Even my uncle knew a lot about him. When I asked, he told me that one of his brothers used to work with Tom. The partnership ended when Tom showed up at a burglary with a small arsenal of weapons. Even the Webb's drew the line at violence. Going to jail for a few months for B and E was one thing. Going to jail for life because a homeowner, cop or innocent bystander was killed was an entirely different ballgame.

The pile of discarded coffee cups and cigarette butts grew bigger. My work didn't get done that day. Not a one of my co-workers was in a position to complain. Their jobs were left unfinished too.

We have all been to funerals where a steady stream of people stand up to praise the good deeds of the recently departed. The next two hours passed in a similar fashion. This gathering of men took turns telling stories about Tom Crawford. By the time we locked up the shop at seven o'clock; normal quitting time was five-thirty, I thought I knew Tom Crawford as well as most people. He wasn't going to be missed even by those he considered friends. Tom owned a vicious temper that would flare up at the least provocation. I heard about the time he put a man in the hospital because he accidentally bumped into him at a pool table. I heard about the time he turned his brother in to the cops for a hundred-dollar reward. I heard about the time he supposedly burned a cop car. I say supposedly because, although a police car burned, the police had no proof that it was Crawford who had torched it. No one else stepped forward to take the credit, so most people grudgingly accepted that it was probably Tom's handiwork. Rumour had it that Tom's own father may have died as the result of one of Tom's beatings. Tom was known to drop off the face of the Earth on occasion. Sometimes, he would be gone for a few days and other times he might be gone for several weeks. No one knew where he went, but he was widely suspected of being a hit man for organized crime.

Tom wasn't the strongest of men. A fourteen-year-old could probably out-box or out-wrestle him, but you didn't get a chance to box or wrestle Tom. He always had the equalizer: a baseball bat, pool cue or a gun. Tom was amoral, fearless and mean. He would steal from you, beat you and then stand in line to pay his respects to your family.

After the last story was told, we locked up and my uncle offered me a ride home. I should have taken him up on his offer, but I was in no hurry to return to an empty house and I had a lot to think about. I wanted to think about Laura. I forgot to get her last name, but thoughts of Tom Crawford and Officer Carruthers kept intruding. I guess I should have been paying more attention to what was going on around me, because I was half-way across a street near my home when I was knocked over by a speeding blue pick-up truck. Dazed I might have been, but I'll swear that the truck did not have its lights on. I tried to read the plate number, but in the darkness that was impossible. I took pride in the fact that I could recognize most vehicles on the road. The truck that nearly ran me over and then failed to stop was a Dodge Ram 150. Although it wasn't new, it was only two or three years old. I picked myself up from the street. The elbow that was already bruised and sore, compliments of Dan Carruthers, had competition for my attention. My shoulder was badly bruised where the truck's mirror hit me. I had an idea I knew what people meant when they talked about road rash. My palms and knees were bleeding from the abrasive pavement.

In retrospect, I was lucky. I could have been killed. If I had not stopped and turned to pick up what I thought was a quarter, I would have been a permanent part of the truck's grill. I still wanted that quarter, so after a careful check for traffic, I again ventured out into the street. It was a slug. You know the kind that comes off electrical boxes. I picked it up and put it in my pocket anyway. I continued down the street at a limping walk, avoiding my usual route. I could see cop cars parked at the scene of last night's fire and I wanted to avoid the cops at all costs. I turned the corner near my home, and sure enough, there was another cop car parked in the street. I snuck down the back alley, opened the back door and without turning on any lights, I heated up a can of soup and prepared for bed. I couldn't remember the last time I went to bed without checking on the Monte Carlo that sat in the garage, so I lifted a corner of the blind to see if the cops were still parked out front. Unfortunately they were still there. The Monte Carlo wouldn't miss my attention for one evening, but I certainly missed attending to the Monte Carlo.

CHAPTER FOUR

I spent another night tossing and turning. The previous night's demons were joined by the day's revelations and new bruises. The combination proved powerful enough to chase away any thoughts of sleep. Ten minutes before the alarm was to go off, I gave up and crawled out of bed. A quick peek through the still-closed blind showed that the police officers were persistent, if nothing else. I opened the fridge and remembered that I was supposed to have picked up groceries the day before. I was forced to make a choice. Eat an apple for breakfast or an apple for lunch. I chose the latter and dropped the apple into my back pack.

Sometime during my feeble attempt at sleep, I made the decision not to hide from the police. If indeed, it was Dan sitting outside in the parked police car, I was going to ignore him. I was ready to leave a good twenty minutes earlier than normal. I walked out the door anyway. I didn't want to be late meeting Laura and what was her name? Oh yeah! Tracy.

I couldn't resist the temptation to glance at my pride and joy in the garage. Two and a half weeks to go! The car was exactly as I left it. Before I could relock the door, I was grabbed roughly by my sore shoulder and spun around. It wasn't Dan but it might have been his twin. I was dragged toward the squad car, and sure enough Dan climbed out of the driver's side door to glare at me. I almost laughed at his appearance. It had been a rough night for me but, at least I was on a half-comfortable bed. Dan and his partner must have spent the night in the close confines of their car. The only thing untidier than their uniforms was their hair. Their eyes were bloodshot and the smell of stale cigarette smoke would haunt me for days.

Dan demanded to know where I had been hiding. I told him the truth. I was in bed. He didn't want to believe me. He saw me walk out the front door with his own eyes but, still he did not want to believe me. "Crawford's dead and you killed him. I can't prove it yet but I will. You and your father better not leave town. We're watching you." After saying that, Dan gave me a shove. It was unexpected and I lost my balance. I would have fallen if Dan's partner hadn't straightened me up with an elbow to my ribs.

With that, they got in the car and drove around the block. I took a look around but if any of the neighbours were aware of the exchange they weren't about to come to my rescue. I found it hard to believe that Dan was willing to sacrifice a good night's sleep to deliver his feeble warning. Was I missing something?

The entire exchange took less than ten minutes. I had a few minutes to spare so I stopped at a donut shop to pick up breakfast. Being as I was such a gentleman, I picked up extra donuts for Laura and Tracy. My timing was perfect. I turned the corner just in time to see Laura turning the corner at the other end of the block. Laura wasn't alone of course, but my puppy-love struck eyes noticed little else. Not even the police car that was idling slowly down the street.

I was tongue-tied as Laura and Tracy approached. If possible, Laura appeared to be almost as shy as I was. She had trouble looking at me when I finally managed to say good morning. I was so flustered that I forgot about the donuts that I carried. Tracy pointed to the bag. "Hey Laura, look, he brought donuts.

Hope you brought chocolate. I love chocolate donuts. Laura's favourite is jam busters. Got any jam busters in there?"

I could not believe my luck. I was not sure what kind of donuts to buy so I opted to buy one of each of my favourites. I had a chocolate-glazed donut, a maple-glazed donut and can you believe it, I had a jam buster. I passed the donuts around and we started on our way.

Left to ourselves, Laura and I would have talked little. Tracy took care of that. She kept up a constant banter. She first asked me about myself and then she persuaded Laura to tell me a little about herself. I was slowly learning about the cousins.

Tracy was carrying a back-pack that appeared to be almost as big as she was. As it looked heavy, I offered to carry it for her. Laura and I both blushed when the little chatter box piped up and said "Hey you big oaf. You'll need one hand to eat your donut and Laura wants to hold the other. How are going to carry my bag too? I'll manage it, thanks."

Carefully wiping my hand on my pants, I dropped it to my side. A few moments later, I felt Laura's long, thin and very warm fingers reaching out. Tracy laughed uproariously. Laura met my sheepish smile with yet another blush. We were still holding hands when we reached the school. Neither of us wanted to let go but, unfortunately the door did not open up by itself. We promised to meet later and went our separate ways. Twenty-five minutes, later I was sitting in Math class and I realized I still did not know Laura's last name.

The morning passed without incident. As I walked by, I heard the same people making the same snide remarks, but today they didn't bother me at all. Laura sat next to me in Science class. The topic that day was lasers. To this day I don't know how lasers work. The class was not a total loss. I learned that Laura's last name is Torino. Her father and Tracy's father were brothers, so I guess that made Tracy's last name Torino as well.

When the lunch bell sounded, we met Tracy at her locker and went outside. Laura offered me a granola bar and Tracy pulled out a bag of oatmeal-raisin cookies not unlike yesterday's cookies. They tasted good so my apple remained in my backpack. With just a little urging from Tracy, Laura opened up towards me for the first time. She started telling stories about her babysitting adventures and before long all three of us were laughing so hard there were tears in our eyes.

The laughter disappeared when we noticed six of the boys from yesterday's encounter coming towards us. We started walking towards a larger group of students that were hanging around the school's front door. We were cut off before we could get anywhere near them. The six boys surrounded us. They took turns telling us what they were going to do to us.

If they were to be believed, it would not be long before I was maimed and killed. One of them showed me the handle of a knife that was sticking out of his pants. Another pulled out a pair of brass knuckles. I was the lucky one.

The boys told Laura and Tracy that they were going to rape, burn and strangle them. Their recital included several lewd demonstrations. We were not a target of opportunity. These boys had put some thought into this. They were careful to shield the one doing the talking and gesturing from anyone else in the area.

Laura was holding tightly onto one of my arms. I kept trying to grab Tracy as well, but she kept moving away. Yesterday, she was right in the middle of things yelling and threatening with the best of them. Today she wasn't saying a thing. She kept fiddling with a gold chain that was hanging around her neck. She appeared to be fidgety. She was turning this way and that always clutching the writing pad to her chest.

While our tormentors were talking, I kept trying to edge the girls toward the other students. I could now see one of the supervisors standing among them and I was hoping to attract someone's attention. I was getting nowhere fast. The boys kept us surrounded. Just when I thought yelling might be my only alternative, they started to give us some room. One of the boys pointed towards the street, and they quickly split up. The quarterback of the football team, the same young man who was the toast of his classmates, the teachers and the alumni turned to us and said "You will get yours. Some day we will catch you alone. There won't always be others around to protect you." He left, and for the first time I noticed that a cop car had pulled up a couple hundred yards away. Thank you, Dan Carruthers, or should I say Officer Carruthers.

It wasn't yet one p.m. and I had been threatened twice already today. At least this time I knew why.

For the first time, I saw Laura crying. Not for herself, but because she thought it was her fault that I was involved. She kept apologizing to me. I spent the rest of the lunch hour telling her about my life, especially the last couple of days. I tried to convince her that I would have attacked a nun for using dirty holy water, or a baby for trying to pull a dog's tail if they had crossed my path. She didn't buy it one hundred percent, but the small smile that crossed her face appealed to me more than her tears.

Tracy listened to everything I said without interrupting. Not one word left her mouth. I hadn't known her long, but what I knew of her told me that she should have been spitting mad. Instead she sat quietly, holding her writing pad and playing with the gold chain around her neck.

We discussed our situation and decided that we had better talk to someone in authority. Instead of going to our first class, the three of us went to the office and asked to speak to the principal. She was attending a conference or something, so we were escorted into the vice-principal's office. In our school, the vice-principal was also the phys-ed teacher. We told him our story and he listened attentively, until we gave him the names of the boys involved. Once he heard those names, his attitude changed. How dare we accuse the school's best athletes and its wealthiest students of such deeds? Where was the proof? Where were the witnesses? Did we know we could be expelled for telling lies?

We left the office. I was mad. I could see more tears in Laura's eyes despite her efforts to hold them back. Tracy still had not said a word. The writing pad was showing signs of wear and her gold chain was now wrapped around her little finger. We were in no mood to face our fellow students this afternoon, so we retraced our steps to the office. The secretary wouldn't let us back in to see the vice-principal, but she was more than happy to have him sign the permission slips we needed to leave school early.

We left the school with no particular destination in mind. I offered to show the girls my Monte Carlo. Without any hesitation what so ever they said "wonderful idea." I was happy for the opportunity to lead the way.

If I learned anything that day, it was to be careful. We were probably safe enough. Dan and his partner should have been sleeping. The kids from school should have been in class. Was I forgetting anyone? Tom Crawford. He was dead, was he not?

We walked by the grocery store and I remembered the empty fridge at home. I excused myself and ran inside. I came outside with some pancake mix, a couple of juice boxes, oranges and pears, bread, sandwich meat and milk.

We passed the burnt-out hulk that used to be Tom Crawford's house. The area was roped off and a fire investigator's vehicle was parked in the driveway. I showed the girls where I had been standing when I saw the man running away and the tracks that Dan made when he needlessly drove up onto Tom's neighbour's lawn. I pointed to the garden hose that I had wielded to virtually no effect. Laura and I followed Tracy when she left the street, walked down a driveway, passed his garage and entered the back alley. She asked me again where I saw the man running. I pointed in the general direction, but when I went to move closer to show her exactly where the runner went, I was waved back. Tracy was scanning the ground carefully. She must have noticed something because she reached into her bag and pulled out an expensive-looking camera. I looked doubtfully at Laura. She shrugged and told me that her uncle - Tracy's Dad - owned an electronics shop. He allowed Tracy to check out the merchandise. According to Laura, Tracy was a wizard when it came to electronics and computers.

At this particular moment, Tracy was busy snapping pictures. She took dozens of pictures, first of the alley itself and then the ground. She reached into her back pack and pulled out a tape measure. She carefully measured the distance between several items on the ground that we could not see from our vantage point. For the first time that day, I saw her open the writing pad. She dug around in her pocket for a few seconds, and then asked if either of us owned a pen that she could borrow. Laura was the first to find one, but when she started to walk towards Tracy, she was asked to stay where she was. "Throw it to me carefully!" Tracy instructed her. "Don't let it hit the ground. I don't want to disturb these tracks."

She made a few notations in the writing pad and then took a minute to look around at some of the surrounding yards. She pointed to a child's sand pail that was lying against a fence and asked me to pick it up. "I'm going to need your pancake mix," she told me. She took the pail and the pancake mix from my outstretched arms, reached into that back pack yet again, and pulled out a bottle of water and another bottle that contained some unidentifiable liquid.

No wonder, that bag was bulky and heavy. I was only half joking when I asked her if there was an X-Ray machine stashed in her bag. She was dead serious when she said, "No, but I have night vision goggles, if we need them." She mixed the concoction together and then poured some of it on the ground. "That'll have to dry for a couple of minutes," she told us.

She handed me the sand pail that was still two-thirds full of paste and once more took up the camera. She walked down the alley towards the street, alternating between scanning the ground and snapping pictures. Twice she bent down, and using a pair of weird-looking pliers that came from – you guessed it – her back pack, she picked up objects and put them in an envelope. She arrived at the street and waved us over. "Stay on the grass. Don't walk in the alley!" were her orders.

She pointed to a couple of tire tracks that were in the dust on the street. "I need more goop to make impressions."

I handed her the bucket after sticking my finger in it. The stuff felt and smelled terrible. I guess I wouldn't be eating pancakes this weekend. Tracy poured my breakfast onto two different tracks and then walked back to her original position to pick up the now dried mixture.

While she was gone, I asked Laura if Tracy did this sort of thing often. Laura shook her head and said, "I've never seen her act like this before. I had no idea she carried all that stuff around with her. I thought it was magazines, or a change of clothes, or something. We watch CSI once in a while, but this; I don't know what this is."

Tracy returned and showed us her handiwork. She held two perfect impressions of the soles of boots. The distinct crack in one of them made me wonder if its owner's sock got wet when it rained. She picked up the tire impressions and carefully wrapped everything, including the envelope into a bundle made from her sweater and placed the bundle in her bag. The moment she swung the bag to her shoulder, the old Tracy returned.

"What do you think? Did I look like an investigator? Did I do a good job? Was I too slow? I always wanted to do this."

The words were spilling out of her. She couldn't keep still. She reminded me of the Looney Tunes cartoon where the young pup kept yapping and bouncing trying to get the attention of the older dog "Spike". Things were back to normal. Laura was smiling. I picked up my bag of groceries, took Laura's hand and started towards home.

The girls shared a canned pop while I put the groceries in the fridge. I checked the house, but as near as I could tell my father still had not been home. I had not seen him for almost a week. Not earth-shattering, in my experience at least, but it would have been nice if he had dropped off a check, or a few dollars to buy food.

Our next stop was the garage. I unlocked the walk-in door, and then threw open the much larger over-head door. I wanted the girls to see my car in the best light possible. Laura appeared to be impressed. She oohed and aahed in all the right places. Tracy on the other hand was just Tracy.

"Has it got a stereo? Can I listen to music? Laura, do you want to listen to music? Is that a CD player? Got any CD's? Wait, I've got CD's in by back pack. I'll bet Malcolm likes heavy metal. How about Black Sabbath or Metallica? I have both.

Yes, the Monte Carlo had a stereo, a very good stereo. One, I had salvaged out of a Mercedes Benz. Yes, I liked heavy metal. Black Sabbath or Metallica would be just fine. We spent the next half-hour listening to music. I was careful to keep the volume low enough so as not to disturb my crotchety old neighbour.

As three-thirty neared, I told the girls that I had to go to work. I would have preferred to stay with them, but as always I needed the money. It was going to cost me a small fortune to license and insure the Monte Carlo. I had some money put away for just that purpose, but if I did not soon hear from my father, I would be using my savings to restock the cupboards that were growing barer each day.

CHAPTER FIVE

The ever-helpful Laura closed the overhead door while I shut off the stereo in the Monte Carlo and retrieved Tracy's CD. I locked the garage door, and then checked to be sure that I had not forgotten to lock the front door of the house. Laura and Tracy were standing at the end of the driveway waiting for me. As I approached them, a blue Dodge truck pulled up beside them. The driver rolled down his window. Guess who stuck his head out? It was none other than Officer Carruthers, still wearing his police uniform.

"Girls," he said. "Did you know that you are hanging out with scum? Webb here is a crook who likes to play with matches. Don't grow too attached to him unless you want to spend your weekends visiting him at the penitentiary." With that, he drove away in a cloud of exhaust.

I apologized to the girls, assuring them that I was not a crook, when Laura piped up, "Please, you don't have to apologize for Dan Carruthers. He did not recognize me, but a few months ago he tried to shake me down. I was leaving an ATM and he drove up beside me. His partner told me to hand over twenty dollars, or I would be accused of shoplifting. I was about to hand it over when a businessman pulled up to the ATM to make a deposit. Rather than be caught out the officers chose to drive off. I didn't report it. Who would I report it to? He belongs in the penitentiary, not you!"

Coming from Laura, it was a long speech and was she angry! Even Tracy was looking at her cousin, surprised at the outburst. If I needed another reason to dislike Dan, I had it. How dare he terrorize young girls, especially the one now holding my hand? We were still standing there, when yet another vehicle pulled up.

I recognized the beat-up old Firebird and its owner. Scott Morgan lived in the area. Our paths crossed many times. You probably could not refer to Scott and me as friends, but we were always civil to one another and often went out of our way to say hello, just as Scott had this afternoon. "Everything o.k., Malcolm," he asked.

I knew Scott had a number of his own problems. Telling him mine would not benefit anyone, so I smiled and told him everything was fine. I introduced him to the Torino cousins. The moment that Tracy heard his last name, another flurry of questions burst out of her.

"Morgan, I know the name Morgan. You're a hero, right? You fought in that war, didn't you? There was a big write-up in the paper about you a month or so back, wasn't there? I told you about it Laura, remember? His foot was ..." She stopped herself before she could finish the sentence. She was horrified because of the mistake she had almost made.

She should not have been. Scott climbed out of the car without showing any signs of resentment. He reached into the back seat for a pair of crutches. "I lost my foot when I stepped on an IED-improvised explosive device," he said while grinning at the much chagrined Tracy. "I get ripped off every time I buy shoes. It does not matter how many times I tell them I only need one, they make me buy two." We all laughed and Tracy relaxed noticeably.

I knew most of Scott's story before I read it in the newspaper. Scott's grandfather was a career soldier and Scott had spent a good portion of his youth listening to the older man's stories of heroism and daring deeds. From an early age, he was taught that he owed his country, his country didn't owe him. The day he turned eighteen, Scott walked into the nearest recruiting office and joined the armed forces. After just a few weeks of training, he was sent to the Middle East. The Middle East was a region in turmoil. Your enemies didn't always wear a uniform, and the children playing on the sides of the road were not always glad to see you.

Two weeks after arriving in the country, Scott was patrolling with his platoon. He saw a group of young boys, ranging in age from about five to ten years old, playing. A soccer ball was sitting on the side of the road. Scott, deciding he wanted to impress the boys, as well as, his fellow soldiers, ran up to the ball and gave it a mighty kick.

He woke up in the infirmary missing a foot. The concussion from the blast knocked him cold. The entire episode was filmed by a news crew that had been given special permission to travel with the platoon. The tape was edited and the portion that showed the young boys laughing at Scott's misfortune didn't make the six o'clock news. The incident was used to teach new arrivals about the dangers they faced.

Scott, not yet nineteen, arrived back in North America. The people, who knew he went to a strange country to protect, not only his country, but mankind in general, called him a hero. He refused to accept their accolades. The people, who believed he was in a strange country fighting an unjust war against people whose only crime was having different beliefs, despised him. He ignored them.

Scott could brush off the accolades and ignore the detractors, but he was disappointed in the politicians who controlled the military purse strings. He understood that he was one of the lucky ones. He came home. Many did not. He listened to politician after politician; in hospitals; at town hall meetings; and even on television talking about the huge sacrifices made by the dead and the wounded to make their country a better place to live. Scott wondered why the politicians wouldn't sacrifice the few extra dollars the dead soldier's families and wounded needed to make their homes a better place to live.

Scott asked what we were up to, so I told him that I was expected at work. I looked at my watch. I needed to be there in seven and a half minutes. "I'll give you a ride. Jump in," he said. I looked towards the girls. Laura whispered in my ear. "Can we trust him?" she asked. I laughed and told her that we could trust him. The beat up old Firebird, I was not so sure about. Tracy piped up, 'I've walked enough for one day so let's go," and climbed into the back seat.

I directed Scott to the corner where the girls and I parted the day before. I helped Tracy climb out of the tiny backseat, but when I reached for Laura's hand to help her, she told me that she wanted to go to the auto wrecker. Who was I to argue? A few minutes later, we pulled up at my place of work. For the second day in a row, I was a couple of minutes late.

I thanked Scott for the ride and made arrangements to meet up with him again in a day or two – the first of many get-togethers. Laura asked where there was a phone she could use to call her parents to let them know where she was. I pointed to the one that sat on the manager's now unoccupied desk. She made her call while I picked up the paperwork that told me what I would be looking for today. By the time we were ready to go to the yard so I could start work, a couple of the other employees returned to the office. My uncle's partner recognized Laura. When he found out she was traveling with me, we were met with a great deal of good-natured teasing. It felt good to be accepted, even by a rag-tag group such as this.

By quitting time, with Laura's help, I had located and removed an entire headlight assembly for a Ford Escort, a rear-door handle for a Nissan Maxima, an ECM for a Chevy Cavalier and a drive-shaft for a Volkswagen Rabbit. Laura was a huge help. I asked her where she learned so much about cars and tools. Her answer, "I spent a lot of time on my grandfather's farm. He was usually fixing something and I liked to help."

Remember, the mangy curs I spoke of earlier. It took weeks before they accepted me. Within minutes, they were literally eating out of Laura's hand. I was impressed and just a little bit jealous. I was getting hungry. I was starving actually, so I assumed Laura was too. I mentioned it to her. She shrugged it off and told me that her older brother would be picking her up in a few minutes to take her home.

Laura gave the dogs one last pet; their tails wagging happily, while I locked the gate. She waved to a young man sitting in a small SUV. "My brother," she said. "He'll give us a ride home. Malcolm, meet my brother Bob. Bob, this is Malcolm." I shook his hand and Bob drove me home by following Laura's instructions.

I appreciated the ride of course, but a few more minutes alone with Laura would have been nearly as nice. Before I got out of the SUV, I made arrangements to meet Laura and Tracy on the way to school the following morning.

The past couple of days were busy ones and I was tired. No lights were on in the house. My father's truck was nowhere to be seen. While I unlocked the house, I was debating on whether or not I should make a few phone calls to try to track him down. Once inside, I noticed that a number of drawers and cupboards had been opened and searched. Even the computer desk had papers strewn all over it. Everything was tidy when I left this morning. What was going on?

I walked into the kitchen and noticed some money sitting on the counter. Two hundred dollars sat there; no note; no explanation; nothing. Dad had paid a visit after all. He must have been in a hurry. Why else would he have not left a note, neglected to pick up the mail that still sat on the table or cleaned up his mess?

I put together a couple of grilled cheese sandwiches. While they were heating up, I tidied up a little and grabbed the mail that was piling up. I threw out the fliers and set the letters addressed to my father aside. I opened the envelopes that looked like they contained bills. Sure enough there was a telephone bill, a bill from the city for trash collection, and of course, there was an electric bill. I ate my sandwiches and set the unpaid bills in the exact spot that I found the money. It was meant as a reminder to my father to pay the bills if he came home again.

I watched television for a while but the two previous sleepless nights caught up with me. Before crawling into the warm bed that beckoned through my bedroom's open door, I lifted a corner of the blind and checked the street. No police car was visible. There were a number of vehicles, but none appeared sinister. Did you think I forgot to check on the Monte Carlo? Not a chance! I had checked on it the moment I got home.

I'd still be sleeping if the alarm's incessant jangling hadn't intruded. Thank goodness! It was Friday. I went through my regular morning routine and left for school. I met Laura and Tracy at the same corner as the day before. It was good to see them again. I didn't wait for an invitation, this morning. I just reached out and took Laura's hand in mine.

I noticed that Tracy's backpack was almost as full as the day before. I asked her what she did with the moulds that she made and the items she picked up in the alley. "They're safe," was all she would say.

We watched carefully as we neared the school. Tracy was walking in front of us and we both saw her stiffen. We followed her gaze and noticed the quarterback locking up a brand new Mustang. I did not think yesterday's goons were serious when they talked about murder and rape, but a beating probably was not out of the question. The bruises and scrapes that I accumulated in the previous few days were still sore, reminding me that a beating would be no fun. What about the girls? What would I do if they tried to hurt the girls? Watching Tracy's back stiffen brought me to a decision. Tonight at work I would find an old fan belt and perhaps the shaft from the inside of a shock absorber. I could easily carry both in my back pack, and if I used them correctly they would make any potential assailant think twice before getting too close. They wouldn't do me any good right now though. I reached for Tracy's arm with my free hand and together we hurried into the school. I don't think the quarterback ever knew we were there.

I escorted first Tracy and then Laura to their homerooms. Once I knew they were safe in their classrooms, I went to my own class.

CHAPTER SIX

A couple of years earlier, one of the tall foreheads that worked in the school division's head office decided that school morale would increase dramatically if regular assemblies, at least twice weekly, were held. In addition, to passing on the latest school news and coming events, the school's brightest students and their best athletes could be singled out as an inspiration to all. He was probably right.

One of his co-workers wrote a paper saying that once a week assemblies were taking up too much of the teachers' and students' time. He was probably right, as well.

A number of studies were conducted, and it was found that it took a minimum of fifteen minutes to assemble five hundred students – the average size of the schools in our district. Add to this, the time it took for the announcements themselves and you could pretty much wipe out half a class. That amount of class time cannot be made up. In addition, it was impossible to determine if students were actually attending the assemblies or if they were skipping out.

Months passed while the school board debated their options. A wealthy alumnus came to their rescue. He offered to provide enough video monitors to equip each class in our school with its own television. It worked great. We heard the announcements, were introduced to the school's most outstanding students and as a bonus, the scores and hi-lights from the school's sports teams could be shown on a continuous loop. The teachers could choose the best times to turn the monitors on. Usually, the best time was at the beginning or end of the class.

Early on that particular Friday morning, the usual announcements were seen and heard. It was during the second class that things grew exciting. Laura and I were sitting at adjoining desks in science class. The teacher gave us our lab assignment and told us to go to work. It was common for this particular teacher to turn on the monitor while we worked, and today was no exception. I was working on my assignment and didn't notice anything unusual until bedlam broke out in the classroom. I looked up and noticed everyone looking at the video monitor. One of the students turned up the volume, and we were all able to see and hear six young men up to no-good. The knife and brass knuckles that I was threatened with the day before were clearly visible. We all heard the threats of rape made against Laura and Tracy. Watching the boys and their gestures might have been funny, if it wasn't for the determined look on their faces and the seriousness of their threats. The three of us at the brunt of the exchange could not be recognized, but it was easy to identify the perpetrators. Laura grabbed my arm. "Tracy," she whispered.

The video ran for about ten minutes, the length of time it took for somebody from the office to notice what was happening, run to the video control room and shut the thing off. Twenty minutes after that, there was a knock at the door of our classroom. The teacher opened it and then beckoned to Laura and me. The vice-principal was standing there, glaring at us. He marched us towards the gymnasium. Why he chose the gym rather than the office was obvious when he shut the door and started yelling at us.

"What are you trying to do, discredit the school? You might have destroyed those boy's lives. How dare you break into the video room? I'll see you charged for that." We let him ramble on. Not once was Tracy's name mentioned, and we certainly were not about to bring it up.

The vice-principal/gym teacher finally ran out of words and offered us the opportunity to defend ourselves. I chose to say nothing. Laura followed suit. I had done nothing wrong and I was sure that at least one other student could vouch for the fact that I had walked directly from one class to the other. Part of the journey was made with Laura at my side, so I knew that they would be unable to pin anything on her either. I kept all this to myself. A little ambiguity right now was a good thing. If they thought I was responsible, they would leave Tracy alone.

The door burst open and our science teacher asked why we weren't in the office. Again, Laura and I opted to remain silent. We merely nodded towards the vice-principal. He was at a bit of a loss to explain the situation. It was his turn to curb his tongue. We followed the teacher to the office. We were met there by a number of others, including the school psychologist, nurse and guidance counsellor.

We told our story for the second time, starting at the beginning by telling them about the cookies and the pony tail episode. We followed that with a report on the previous day's incident, including our visit to the vice-principal. He was going to deny our visit, but Laura glanced towards the outer office where the secretary, who could confirm our version of the facts, sat. I reminded him of the absentee slip that he signed. We did not mention nor were we asked about the origin and playing of today's video.

We were asked if we were hurt in any way. What did we want the school to do about the boys? Did we want the police involved? Did we want to press charges? The guidance counsellor asked our ages, and when they realized albeit belatedly that we were minors, a meeting was arranged that would include our parents, the principal, the school superintendent and a police officer, if we so desired. We were excused until the meeting on Monday. We left the office through a side door so that the six boys who now waited in the outer office could not see us.

At lunch time, we met Tracy at her locker. We opted to go for a walk to a nearby park rather than hang around the school. The Mustang that drew Tracy's attention earlier that day was no longer in the parking lot. Maybe the quarterback and his friends were suspended for the day. Not, if the vice-principal had anything to do with it.

We asked Tracy how she managed to pull off this morning's caper. She showed us where a miniature camera was imbedded in her writing pad. We knew where to look but it was still invisible. The only indication of its existence was the slight bump you felt when you ran your thumb over it. "The chain," I said. "There's a microphone in your chain right."

Tracy giggled and brought the chain out of her pocket. What at first appeared to be a locket was actually a recording device complete with an on/off switch that Tracy demonstrated for us.

"I recorded everything they said and did," she told us. "I spent last night doing some editing and making a DVD. This morning I waited until the second class was about to start and I excused myself to use the washroom. The video room door was open so I went in and put my DVD in the machine. The rest is history. I am surprised nobody suspected us."

We told her about our adventures. She was appalled at the trouble she had caused us. We assured her that we were in no trouble at all. "As a matter of fact," I said, "I think it was for the best. Well, it will be if I can convince my father to attend the meeting."

The afternoon passed without incident. Most of the students were unaware of our involvement in the altercation that was shown in such vivid clarity. Other than a couple of snide remarks regarding my heritage, I was left alone. The school day finally ended and the weekend began.

Weekends for me meant working at the auto wrecker's. Today, I only planned to put in a couple of hours. I was on my way to the wrecker's, Laura beside me and Tracy bouncing along in front. "Mom is making pizza for supper. Mom makes the greatest pizza. I love mushroom, bacon and pepperoni. She smothers it with cheese too, three kinds." Tracy's words were making me hungry.

"Want to go to the show tonight? Did you know Laura's dad owns a movie theatre? Does that robot movie start tonight? I love robots. I can bring one of Mom's pizzas and we can eat it on the way. Laura, do you think we can go to the movie?" Tracy was talking so fast, I don't know how she managed to breathe.

I did not know that Laura's family owned a theatre. There was a lot I didn't know about Laura. Not surprising really. Up until three days ago, I had never spoken to the girl. Right now, she was holding my hand and looking endearingly at me. "Will you come to the show with us?" she asked. "My aunt's pizzas really are to die for."

What could I say? At that moment my three favourite things in life were pizza, movies and Laura. I would apologize to the Monte Carlo later. We made plans to meet outside Tracy's house at six-thirty.

Things were slow at work and I finished up with a few minutes to spare. I noticed my uncle drive up and park. I wanted to ask him if he knew anything about my father's where-a-bouts so I walked over to meet him. He told me that the last time he talked to my father was several days ago. I asked him if he was aware of any of dad's plans. I didn't believe him when he denied any such knowledge; he refused to even look in my direction,

That night, we ate the pizza while sitting on a bench outside the movie theatre. It was very good, especially the cheese. The show wasn't scheduled to start for another forty-five minutes and already a crowd was gathering. Laura told us that she planned to help in the concession area for a little while. Tracy volunteered to join her. I looked at the grease stain on the palm of my hand and the dirt under my fingernails. The concession stand was no place for me. I asked how I could help but was assured that my help was unnecessary. I could find us a seat inside, or if I preferred, I could wait in the lobby. I opted for the lobby.

Maybe Laura was a little shy at school, but she knew what she was doing in the movie theatre. She bounced from one place to another, helping out anyone who fell behind. When the popcorn machine acted up, it was Laura they called for. Without a moment's hesitation she opened an access panel, reached in, grabbed a handful of wires, reconnected two of them, replaced the panel and restarted the machine. It was Laura they called when the soda tanks needed replacing. It was Laura they called when the person selling tickets needed a break. She was even called to help the projectionist set up his machine. I was a little surprised to see this take charge attitude coming from Laura, who until now, always appeared to be bashful. I could learn to like this girl.

A young boy was bumped and accidentally spilled a large glass of Coke. I noticed a mop in a corner behind the counter. I grabbed it and began cleaning up the mess. Laura smiled in my direction and a man, who looked like he might be her father, nodded his appreciation.

It was a full house. We were not paying customers so we chose to watch the film from the projector room. That vantage point proved to be a good one. The movie was alright. The robots cavorted. The aliens caused havoc, and of course, the good guys won.

Once the movie was over, we helped clean up the theatre. It was a learning experience for me. Cleaning up after large crowds was a challenge. We swept up boxes and boxes of spilled popcorn. We filled bag after bag with empty drink cups and candy bar wrappers. Every seat had to be checked and wiped down. It was nothing new to the Torino family and their employees. They took it all in stride. A half hour later, we were all sitting in the family mini-van on our way to enjoy a late night ice-cream cone.

I was right about the man who nodded to me earlier. He was indeed Laura's father, Terry. Laura introduced us at the first opportunity. He took a good hard look at me. I'm sure he recognized the Webb name, but his warm and pleasant manner proved that he wasn't going to hold my name against me. According to Laura, her mother usually accompanied them to the theatre. Tonight, however, she suffered from a migraine and remained at home. "You'll like her", Tracy assured me. "Aunt Becca is a great lady. She has the bluest eyes and a great sense of humour.

We finished our ice cream and the Torino family dropped me off at home. Tracy pointed out the scene of the fire and murder as we drove by. A short discussion on the futility of crime ensued. It was a general discussion. In no way was it directed at me. All in all, it was a pleasant evening. The Torino's were a close knit and friendly family. They made me feel right at home.

My neighbourhood was peaceful. Nothing appeared out of the ordinary. The Monte Carlo was in great shape. In two weeks and two days, I would be old enough to drive it. The house was empty. The pile of bills still sat where I left them. I checked but no money was to be found. Before calling it a day, I took a few minutes to make plans for the next day.

CHAPTER SEVEN

I woke up on Saturday to a beautiful summer day. As I wasn't expected at the auto wrecker's until after lunch, I spent a few minutes luxuriating in the comfort of my bed. It seemed like a good time to try and organize my thoughts. Was it Tom Crawford I saw running away? The more thought I put in to it, the less sure I felt. So what if it was Tom? I told the police what I saw. Was it not their problem now?

What about the police? Where did Joe Grosjean fit in? Should I be more worried about Dan Carruthers and his interest in me? In the three days since the fire, Dan had warned me to watch myself three times. Joe's explanation at the fire scene no longer held much water. The solution seemed simple. If I conducted my life the same way I always had, Dan would have no reason to harass me. Just the same, I decided that it was in my best interest to be wary of Dan and his partner.

Then, there was the incident at school. Thanks to Tracy, we could probably put that event behind us. On Monday, the meeting would take place and all should be settled. I was willing to forget it if the others were.

Tracy! What a friend she was turning out to be? Who was I kidding? It was Laura I wanted to think about. Was it possible that I had a girlfriend? A week ago I would have laughed at the suggestion, but now I could only hope.

As pleasant as the thoughts of Laura were, it was time to get moving. First on my agenda was to try and locate my father. I needed to tell him about the school meeting. Maybe, I would even admit I missed him a little.

Then I remembered the truck that nearly ran me over. With everything else going on the past few days, I almost forgot about that truck. Was being busy, a good enough excuse to forget about it? Wasn't I still aching from the bruises? Whatever the reason, I was going to learn from my mistake; a healthy, happy and prosperous future might depend on it.

While I ate my toast, I made a number of phone calls to relatives, friends and acquaintances of my father. I was still unable to locate him, so I continued by calling his girlfriends, past and present. Nobody knew where he was, or if they did, they weren't telling me. I believed the former. Everyone that I talked to seemed surprised that I had not heard from him. For the first time, I began to be worried. Not so much about the upcoming meeting, but about my father's well-being.

I remembered my conversation with my uncle the day before. I also remembered that I didn't entirely believe his story. He was my next call. At first, my uncle gave me the same song and dance as he had the day before. I don't know where he is. I don't know what he was up to. I persisted and something in my voice must have scared my uncle because he finally opened up, not about my father's whereabouts, but about his plans.

The last time my uncle talked to my father was the day before the fire, two days after I last saw him. They met for coffee and my father had told him a few things in confidence, the sort of things that only brothers, whether brothers by blood, or brothers in crime, would tell one another.

My father was planning a big score. It was to be his biggest ever and if all went according to plan, it would be his last. The plans were well underway and the day of the theft, though not yet confirmed, was imminent. That's all my uncle knew.

I asked who was in on the scheme with my father. "I don't know," said my uncle.

"What are they going to steal," I wanted to know?

"No idea," was the simple response.

I asked my uncle why Dad wasn't keeping in touch with me. "I am a little surprised that he hasn't called you, so I can only guess at the answer to that question," he replied. "It's because of who you are. You are a straight shooter, as honest as they come. Your father, though not as honest, is a man with a strong moral character. He will do anything to protect your reputation. The less you know about his shenanigans the better."

I suppose it made sense. I told my uncle about the grocery money on the counter. "There you go. He hasn't forgotten about you. Everything will work out," he told me.

It was easy for him to say, but not as easy for me to accept. Maybe my father was safe and unharmed, but the fact he was planning a crime worried me almost as much. I mentioned the upcoming school meeting. His answer was typically Webb. "I'll take his place. The school will never know the difference."

I thanked him for the offer, but declined. I hoped to find a better solution. After promising to behave - the request, coming from my uncle was an absolute hoot - I hung up the phone. My next call was to my mother. She sounded happy to hear from me. It was the first time that we had talked in several days.

Our conversation lasted half an hour. I only told her what I felt she needed to know. We talked about school and the upcoming meeting. I mentioned nothing about the fire or my father's disappearance. I couldn't resist telling her about my new friends, Laura and Tracy. She caught on right away and asked which one was my girlfriend. I initially denied the girlfriend part, but after some good natured ribbing I admitted that I really liked Laura.

When at last we hung up the phones, I felt much better about Monday's meeting. I had in my possession all the information I needed to reach my mother at her place of employment. She assured me that she had access to conference calling, video telephones, fax machines and computers. She would be by my side no matter which means of communication the school chose.

My last call of the morning was to Scott Morgan. When we last spoke, I agreed to meet him for hot chocolate sometime this morning. I called him now to see if his offer was still good. The phone rang twice before I heard his always cheerful voice. "Just waiting for your call," was his answer to my question. "I'll be by to pick you up in ten minutes."

I enjoyed the next hour immensely. Scott was fun to be around. Everyone who walked into the coffee shop recognized him and said hello. On the other hand, the few who recognized me passed by without acknowledging my presence!

Scott talked about his plans to open a newsstand in the mall. He grew more and more excited as he described it to me. He had negotiated a lease for a small area near the food court. He hoped to sell newspapers, magazines, candy bars, chewing gum, souvenirs and lottery tickets.

"Why start a newsstand?" I asked him.

"I need a job," he told me. "The army doesn't pay enough for me to live alone. I don't want to sponge off my parents forever. I'd like to have a place to call my own."

"I can't get a regular job. My leg hurts if I stand too much. The stump hasn't healed enough for prosthesis and according to the doctors it won't be healed for quite some time. I don't want to work at a desk or be stuck in a wheel chair. A newsstand should be perfect. Two or three strides and I can get from one side to other. If worse comes to worse, I could roll myself in an office chair. I would be out meeting people and hopefully making a few dollars." He was laughing uproariously when he said, "Most important of all, it won't cost an arm and a leg." He pointed down and said, "As you can see I'm a little short."

Scott insisted on driving me to work. The Firebird started but barely. I was trying to close my door without slamming it – I was afraid it would fall off the hinges if I slammed it too hard – when I noticed Officer Carruthers and his partner sitting in their squad car in the drive-through lane. I noticed Dan writing in his notebook. I hoped he wasn't writing down Scott's plate number so that he could harass him later. Dan was putting his notebook in his pocket when his partner nudged his arm. I watched as they both turned and looked at a blue truck parked on the other side of the street.

We all know there is nothing suspicious about cops with coffee, donuts and a drive – through, so I returned my attention to the door that still wasn't closed. "Lift it a little and pray. Sometimes that works," said Scott when he noticed my predicament. I lifted and said a small prayer. The door closed with a nice satisfying clunk and I forgot all about the incident.

The wrecking yard was usually a busy place on Saturdays. Today was no exception. As soon as I arrived, I was handed my weekly pay check. Five hours later, I still had not had a chance to see if it was correct. The weekend do-it-yourself crowd was out in full force. They told me what they wanted and it was my job to show them where it was. I was constantly on the go. Ford Taurus' were over here. Chevrolet Impalas were out back. There's a Dodge 300 sitting over there. Yes! The right rear door is good. Sorry! We crushed the last Honda Civic last week. We have a 2004 Lexus. Let me check to see what model it is. On and on it went. I was exhausted when I closed the gate at five-thirty p.m.

Tracy and Laura were waiting in the office for me. I was expecting them. We planned it before we went our separate ways the previous evening. Even so, I half-expected them to be no-shows. It was tough to outgrow insecurity. I was excited to see them. I counted up my tips for the day – thirty-five dollars. Maybe, I wasn't so exhausted after all. Another look at the girls and I knew I wasn't ready to call it a day.

The mall was only a few blocks away and the weather was still nice, so we opted to walk rather than accept the ride that one of my co-workers offered. We paid a visit to the food court and ordered tacos, two for me, one for each of the girls. Any other time, I would have eaten three of the tasty little morsels. Today, I was out to make an impression. Wow, was my life changing or what?

We wandered up one aisle and down another. I found one of my bank's ATM's and deposited my pay check. Money wasn't going to be a problem for a few weeks at least.

I told the girls about Scott and his newsstand. We tried to figure out where it was going to be located, but I wasn't even sure we were in the right mall. It wasn't long before we found ourselves in a store that sold video games. We had to wait our turn, but eventually we were able to play a couple of games on the store's equipment.

For the first time that day I thought about the Monte Carlo that was sitting in the garage waiting for me to drive it. To drive it, I would need a licence. To get a licence, I would need practice. I asked the clerk if they had any games that simulated driving. He came up with two. We used our allotted time trying them out. Laura too, would soon be trying to get her licence. We took turns driving the various cars through the game's mazes. There was little to choose between us. Just as we were finishing up, Tracy asked for a turn. She blew us away. She drove twice as fast and made half the mistakes. We all laughed about it, but in truth I was a little embarrassed. I was male. I was older. It was, after all cars. Shouldn't I have been embarrassed?

Despite my bruised ego I had a good time. Fast food, video games and the mall – what teenager would not be having fun?

It was Tracy's family's turn to pick us up. Did these girls have it made it or what? They had parents, aunts and uncles, even brothers and sisters at their beck and call. Need a ride? Pick up the phone and one is on the way.

Today it was Tracy's mother, Gladys who picked us up. After the obligatory introductions, we were off. Instead of stopping for ice cream, she drove to one of those frozen yogurt places. It wasn't shyness, or fear of gaining weight that forced me to decline her offer of buying me yogurt. I don't like yogurt. I don't care if it's frozen, plain or fruit-filled. I hate the smell, texture and taste of the stuff. I was far too polite to tell Gladys, so I let her believe I was still full from the tacos.

Another driver meant another trip past the scene of the fire. Once more, I found myself telling a sympathetic adult about my part in the drama. It's too bad the sympathetic adult wasn't my father. The darkness of the house when Mrs. Torino parked in front of it told me that he would not be hearing my story tonight. Ah well! I'll save that for a therapy session.

I jumped out of the van. I was heading up the drive when Laura rolled her window down and told me to be ready at ten the following morning. She had a surprise for me. We would be gone most of the day. I love surprises, so I assured her I would be ready.

I checked the street. Everything looked normal. I checked the Monte Carlo. It was in fine shape. I checked the inside of the house. It was undisturbed.

I dug around for something to eat and finally decided on a can of pasta. There were no girls watching me now so I ate the entire can. Sometimes change isn't easy.

The butt-kicking I took from Tracy earlier was still on my mind so I went on-line and spent an hour and a half studying for the written portion of my driver's test. By then I was truly exhausted so I crawled into bed. I heard nothing until the alarm went off at nine a.m.

CHAPTER EIGHT

By ten o'clock the following morning I was awake, showered and dressed in my best casual clothes. Earlier that morning, I decided to do a load of laundry. I knew it was time to do laundry when the pile of clothes on the bedroom floor was larger than the pile of clothes in my closet. This morning the only clothes in my closet were the jeans I was wearing and a bathrobe. Now there was a load of laundry in the dryer and another in the washing machine. I still had a few minutes to spare so I started a grocery list. Most of the money that I found sitting on the counter was in an envelope in my sock drawer for safe-keeping. Judging by the list in front of me that was long and growing longer, my next trip to the grocery store would make keeping it safe unnecessary. I remembered the near empty laundry detergent bottle and the list grew longer still.

For what seemed liked the thousandth time, I looked out the window. This time, I was rewarded when I noticed the now-familiar minivan pull up. I was on my way out the door before they even had time to honk their horn. I was almost running down the step when I ran into Laura. I mean, I literally ran into her. We both fell down from the impact. I was mortified. A big clumsy oaf like me running into a frail, skinny wisp of smoke like Laura. There could be only one outcome, couldn't there? Laura picked herself up, gave me a peck on the cheek and smiled.

"Bring a bathing suit," she said. "I forgot to tell you last night."

It took me more than a few seconds to react. Instead of seeing tears at best and broken bones at worst, Laura greeted me with a peck and a smile. Only when she told me to hurry did I regain my senses. I unlocked the door and went inside to retrieve my swimming trunks. I don't know why. I wouldn't be putting them on. If I wasn't ready to let her watch me eat three tacos, then I wasn't ready to let her see my pasty white and bloated body in a swim suit.

Twenty minutes later, we were out of the city and enjoying the bright green countryside. Laura's parents', Terry and Becca sat in the front. Her brother Bob sat in the back row and listened to music on an I-pod. Laura and I sat in the middle row. It was the first time I had met Becca. Now I knew where Laura got her looks. Like her daughter, Becca was tall and slender. She had the same pale complexion and long black hair. Laura was a great looking girl and if her mother's looks were any indication, she was going to be an even better looking woman.

The old insecurities tried to take over once more. She's too good for me. What could she possibly see in me? What did a kid like me, from the wrong side of the tracks, have to offer a pretty girl with a well-adjusted family? I looked towards Laura. I saw nothing but tenderness in her eyes and a smile on her face; all directed at me. Life was good.

I asked where we were going and was ignored by the entire Torino family. They acted like they never heard my question. I really didn't need to know. If you're enjoying the journey, what difference does the destination make, right? After several minutes of small talk and friendly banter the subject of Tom Crawford came up.

For several days now, the news was full of stories about Tom and the fire. The first stories described the details of the fire and the body found in the basement. By the third day when no new details were forthcoming, the stories were more speculation than hard facts. The body was now undergoing DNA testing to determine its identity. The process normally took several days to complete – hard to believe that just a few short years ago it often took months to conduct the same tests. Because of the lack of a positive identification, there was some speculation on the body's identity. There was loads of speculation about the cause of the fire. One reporter quoted a reliable source who said that the fire was a result of a meth lab mishap. Yet another reliable source said Tom was killed when the bomb he was building exploded. Channel six's news lady told her audience that a fire investigator's report indicated that the fire was started with gasoline. One newspaper article said that the fire occurred because of an electrical short.

My name didn't appear anywhere, thank heavens. There were several reporters on site while I was sitting in Dan's police cruiser but, apparently none of them took note of me. The closest anyone came to mentioning me was the reporter who said that a suspect was detained and then released at the scene of the crime. Why no one chose to expand on this statement was a mystery to me. It was a mystery that I hoped wasn't solved.

Murder, accidental death, or death by misadventure, the police weren't talking. They weren't talking about the man I saw either. Either they didn't believe me, or they were withholding that information. I was betting they didn't believe me.

The Torino's asked my opinion on the whole scenario. They were being polite. I really don't think they expected me to have an opinion one way or another. I told them what I thought they expected me say. No matter how he died, Crawford probably deserved it.

With that touchy subject out of the way – touchy for me anyway – we embarked on an even touchier subject, tomorrow's meeting at the school. We had to decide what we felt would be adequate punishment for our tormentors. We also had to decide what to do about Tracy. She was as much a victim as the rest of us and she and her parents deserved some say in how it was resolved. Our silence on Friday denied them that opportunity.

Laura felt as I did regarding punishment. As long as we were left alone, we really didn't care what happened. Laura's parents respected our decision and it was decided that we would leave the punishment up to the school. We would not press for criminal charges. As for Tracy and her parents, we decided to let them decide if they wanted to join us at the meeting. It would be tough for the school to punish her, or us, for that matter, for broadcasting the incident, especially after we told them about the vice-principal's threats.

Thirty minutes from the city's outskirts, we turned down a much-traveled gravel lane. We pulled up in front of a large comfortable looking country home. The yard was well kept with a big red barn, two long machine sheds and a number of other outbuildings. We weren't the first arrivals. A number of other vehicles were already parked in the yard including the van that Tracy's mom used to drive us home the night before. This must be the farm that was owned by Laura's grandparents.

Laura confirmed it when she said, "What do you think? This is my grandparent's. I love coming out to the farm. This is only part of the surprise. After brunch I'll show you the rest of it."

I walked into the house with the rest of Laura's family. There had to be at least a dozen people sitting at the dining room table. There was room for at least a dozen more. This house was designed for entertaining guests. If its present occupant's familiarity with the place was any indication, they entertained often. Laura took me around the room making introductions. Uncle this, aunt that, cousin so and so; I couldn't remember them all. Before she was finished, another vehicle pulled into the yard and the introductions started over. Tracy, of course, was there. Any doubts that Laura wasn't her favourite cousin were put to rest when she made a beeline towards us as we entered the house, and then never left Laura's side.

I noticed something about the girls that day. Laura was just as active and vivacious around her family as she was in the movie theater. Tracy, on the other hand, who until now, always seemed to me to be the life of the party, took a back seat to her older cousin. There was no doubt that Laura was the leader.

Some of Laura's relatives appeared to be wealthy, some, like her parents were definitely middle-class, and judging by the vehicles they drove and the clothes they wore, a couple of her cousins were probably not very well off. Despite their financial means, they all had a few things in common. They were all friendly, cheerful, outgoing; and all brought food.

Brunch consisted of pancakes, French toast, ham, bacon, sausages, omelettes, fruit slices of all kinds, bread, obviously homemade, and hash browns. If that wasn't enough, plate after plate of desserts was placed on the table. Best of all, I could dig in. I looked at everybody else filling their plates to overflowing and felt right at home.

Lunch was a long and drawn-out affair. When we were finished eating, pots of tea, coffee and hot chocolate were set on the table. We all helped ourselves. There had to be at least ten different conversations going on at the same time. Nothing was taboo. Politics, religion, business and current affairs were all on the agenda. Not all conversations were serious. The patriarch of the family, Laura and Tracy's grandfather, was busy telling jokes at one end of the table. They must have been pretty good jokes because everyone within ear-shot was killing themselves laughing. About twenty people were sitting in that dining room, and unlike the Webb family gatherings, there wasn't a frown or look of displeasure to be seen. Also, unlike Webb gatherings, I doubt if anyone present was on the run from the law.

One of the older men announced it was time to stretch his legs. Just like that, everyone pushed back their chairs, and prepared to leave the table. Everybody, young, old and in between chipped in to help clean up. Ten minutes later, it was done and people scattered. Some went to change into swimsuits, some sat on the deck and smoked, a few went to the basement to play games and some chose to wander around outside.

Laura grabbed my hand, and with Tracy right behind us, led me outside where her grandfather waited. The four of us climbed into his pickup and he drove to another yard-site a couple of miles away. The buildings in this yard were well-kept but weren't as immaculate as the ones we just left. To my surprise, there was an obstacle course set up in an adjoining field. There was a place for parallel parking, and a place for backing up, but most of the course involved manoeuvring around a wide variety of objects.

This was Laura's surprise and I was truly impressed. I could hardly wait for the opportunity to show my stuff. The course looked easy. There was tons of room to get around. An old half-ton truck sat in a lean-to and I assumed we would be driving it. Instead, the elder Torino pulled up beside a big old grain truck. "You want to learn to drive, son? Out here you learn the hard way. When you can drive this monster through that course you'll be able to drive anything, even that sports car that Laura tells me you've been working on."

The obstacle course, that a moment ago seemed so huge, now looked a whole lot smaller. I was sceptical, but with Tracy and Laura's encouragement I decided to give it a shot. Mr. Torino showed me how to drive the big truck. He told me how to shift the gears in its manual transmission and how to make the best use of the rear view mirrors. I took the wheel and drove slowly to a wide-open field where I practiced driving and shifting. It wasn't as hard as I thought it might be and before long I was told to try out the obstacle course. That was a challenge.

The truck was big. It didn't turn very sharp and you couldn't see a thing behind you. If I tried to go too slow, the fool truck stalled out on me. I practiced and I was getting better. Clutch; brake; step on the gas just a little; watch the rear view mirror; I was getting the hang of it. Soon it was time for me to take a break so Laura climbed into the driver's seat.

She had trouble getting used to shifting the gears but eventually she too was ready for the obstacle course. She made several passes at it and eventually managed to complete the course. It was time for our road test.

Mr. Torino told us we had three minutes to complete the course without running into anything. It took me two minutes and fifty-five seconds but on my second try I passed. It took Laura four tries and three minutes and ten seconds to complete the course without a mistake. It had been a challenge and we were proud to be able to say that we mastered it.

While we were driving, Tracy was busy replacing the barrels, pylons and other obstacles that we had knocked over with the truck's heavy bumpers. We kept her busy, but not so busy that she couldn't find the time to heckle us about our mistakes. Every time we hit something, we could hear her laughter and wise cracks through the open window of the truck.

When we were finished, Laura insisted that Tracy take a turn. I was worried. I remembered what had happened in the video store when Tracy out-drove both of us. I needn't have worried. Tracy couldn't drive the big truck. She couldn't even steer a wheelbarrow. Nobody would steer the wheelbarrow that used to sit in an out-of-the-way corner near a tool shed, because Tracy ran over it. It was a miracle that she missed the tool shed. Apparently, steering a video controller was a lot easier than steering a grain truck. Tracy never did get the hang of the truck. We were relentless in our teasing. To shut us up, she jumped on an ATV in an effort to beat our time through the obstacle course. She took off in reverse and ran over my foot. She never did make it through the obstacle course.

We returned to the main house. The girls went for a swim while I joined a couple of the guys in a game of billiards. The afternoon passed quickly and before I knew it we were called to supper. Barbecued steaks, ribs, pork chops and chicken all sat on a table outside. Another table was full of salads. Lettuce salads, potato salad, green bean salad and a couple of salads I had never seen before. Did I mention the buns? Of course they were home - made.

Before we left to return to the city, we had a brief chat with Tracy and her parents. Tracy insisted, and her parents agreed, that she should tell the school officials about her role in broadcasting the video. She didn't want Laura or me to be accused of something we didn't do. Other than that they felt the same way towards the culprits as the rest of us. Let the school punish them as they saw fit. It was agreed that they would join us at tomorrow's meeting.

It was a quiet trip back to the city. Fresh air; good company; great food; we were all too tired for anything but small talk. Movies were the main topic of discussion. As you would expect from a family that operated a movie theatre they knew a lot about movies and movie-making. Laura amazed me with her knowledge. Her parents let her answer all of my numerous questions. Not once did they find it necessary to correct her.

CHAPTER NINE

The alarm blasting in my ear told me it was Monday morning. Monday's were relentless. They arrived whether we were ready for them or not. I suppose I was ready for this one. Time would tell.

I had arrived home well after dark, the night before. A week ago, I never would have paid attention to what was happening on the street, but now the first thing I did when nearing my home was to check for strange vehicles. Everything appeared normal. The house was just as I left it which meant there was no news from my father. Up until that moment, I was still hoping he would be around to attend the school meeting. The realization that he wouldn't be there hurt a little, but it was nothing a tough independent Webb couldn't handle. I folded that morning's laundry and put it away before going to bed.

Now it was time to start a new day and a new week. Have a shower; make breakfast; put a sandwich together for lunch; you know the routine. I went through it all before heading off to meet Laura and Tracy on our way to school.

As the meeting wasn't scheduled until two that afternoon, we spent the morning attending our usual classes. Laura and I compared notes in Science class and we determined that our assailants weren't in school that morning. To the dismay of our fellow students, the monitors in the classrooms remained silent. If you wanted to find out who won that weekends volleyball tournament, you had to check the bulletin board near the gym. The student, who won the city-wide chess tournament and the two young ladies who beat out six other teams to win a debating contest, would have to wait one more day for their accomplishments to become known.

At lunch time, the three of us left the school property. All morning we heard the whispers behind our backs. The rumour mill was in full force. To avoid having to answer any questions, we decided to just leave. When the bell rang, we were the first ones out the door. We ate our sandwiches and drank our juice while sitting on a curb in a residential neighbourhood near the school.

The hour between one and two seemed to take forever. My grandfather often talked about having ants in one's pants. Maybe the saying was old and out of date, but I couldn't think of a better way to describe the way I felt. Despite knowing I did nothing wrong, I was worried. I had the Webb reputation against me. The vice-principal/gym teacher made it clear he was against us. What would the others think? At ten minutes to two, I was excused from class. I met Tracy, Laura and their parents in the hallway outside the office. I checked my pocket one more time to make sure I had the phone numbers to reach my mother. They were still there, but if I kept folding and unfolding the piece of paper they were written on with my sweaty fingers it might just disintegrate.

I thought we would all be called in together, but to my chagrin we were called in separately. Mine was the first name called. I entered the principal's office. I was greeted by the principal. The school psychologist was there and so was the guidance counsellor. The vice-principal wasn't, but in his place was a familiar face. I wasn't surprised to see a police officer because we were told on Friday to expect one. I was a little surprised to see Joe Grosjean, but come to think of it why shouldn't he be there. The school was a part of his beat. Would I have preferred to see Dan Carruthers? Yeah! Right!

Joe stood and shook my hand. "Good to see you Malcolm," he said, before the principal had time to introduce us. "We met on another matter," he informed the others in the room.

I was asked why my parents weren't present. I didn't want to explain about my father, so I told them he was unavailable and offered them my mother's phone number. The call was put through, and within three minutes everyone in the room could see my mother's image on a teleconferencing screen. Introductions were made and I was encouraged to tell my story. I told it the way I remembered it without embellishing or whitewashing anything. I told them that Tracy was with me, as well as, Laura in an attempt to explain her and her parents' presence in the outer office. I told them about the knife that was dropped, but I didn't tell them that Tracy had picked it up. I didn't tell them about Tracy's recording devices. That was best left for her to explain. When I was asked if I wanted to press charges, I looked toward Joe and said, "No. As long as I am left alone and no longer tormented, I am content to let the school handle the discipline."

As one the room's occupants turned to the screen to see my mother's reaction. She responded immediately, "I'm with Malcolm. If that's what he wants, I won't argue."

The principal thanked us for our time and asked me if I would hang around until they finished talking to the others. Who was I to argue? I said goodbye to my mother and blushed when she blew me a kiss in front of the others.

Laura and her parents were invited into the office next. I sat next to Tracy while we waited for the interview to conclude. Tracy wanted to talk about my meeting, but even though I wasn't specifically instructed not to say anything, I believed we would all be better off if what we said didn't sound rehearsed.

We wound up talking about movies, music and television. Did you know that two well-known singers were divorcing and fighting over custody of their children? Thanks to Tracy, we knew.

In what seemed like hours, but in reality was only twenty minutes; Laura walked out of the office and sat down beside me. She was joined by Terry and Becca a minute later. Terry playfully slapped my shoulder as he walked by. "Good job," he said.

I appreciated his support a lot more than I can say in a few words. Once the second Torino family was out of earshot in the principal's office, we talked about the testimony we gave. To no one's surprise, our stories were almost identical. With that out of the way, our conversation turned to other things: television, movies and music. I started to tell them about the two singers. "We know," they said in unison. We all laughed.

Eventually, Tracy returned to her seat beside me. She appeared to be much chastised. Her father joined us and told us what happened. Tracy told pretty much the same story as we did. Then she admitted to picking up the knife. When prodded, she dug the knife out of her bag and handed it over to Joe. She dug a little deeper into her bag and came up with the camera and recording device. She admitted that it was her who had made the recording and subsequent DVD - the same DVD that now sat on the principal's desk - the DVD that backed up much of what we said. For her trouble, Tracy received a severe scolding. She had to promise the school and her parents that she would make no more recordings without permission. She had to promise to stay out of the school's video control room. Joe gave her a lecture about withholding evidence and carrying dangerous weapons.

When we heard the news, Laura and I promised to help keep Tracy out of trouble. Then we were all called back into the inner office. The room was full. In fact, it was overflowing. A room that was designed to sit six people at the most, now held eleven. The adults sat; the principal on the corner of her desk and Joe on a box in a corner; while Tracy, Laura and I stood. I was asked if I wanted them to call my mother. I remembered the blown kiss and declined their offer.

Joe was the first to speak. He told us that we had more than enough evidence to press charges against our assailants. Even if we didn't have the video, he was sure we could make the charges stick. With the video, it was a no-brainer. He could proceed without us, but probably would not. He asked us once more if we wanted to lay charges. He looked at each of us in turn, including the parents. We all said no. He duly recorded our answers in a notebook. If we changed our minds, we were to call him. He told us that he was taking the knife and video with him as evidence. He made a show of handing the principal a receipt for the items; she in turn made a show of making a new file to hold the receipt.

He told us that it was his job to speak to each of the young men involved, telling them that they would be lucky to avoid jail time and that he would come looking for them if any harm came to us, whether they were responsible or not. Before he excused himself, he spent a few moments talking about statutes of limitations, citizen's rights and other legal mumbo-jumbo that I didn't understand.

Once Joe left the room, the subject of the vice-principal and his actions came up. I did most of the talking. When I was finished Laura and Tracy gave their take on the situation. Our statements were written down by the guidance counsellor and after reading it over one last time, each of us signed it. The principal assured us that his behaviour would be brought to the attention of the school board.

By now, the over-crowded room was stifling hot. To my embarrassment, sweat was dripping off my brow and the wet spots under my arms were growing. I looked around the room to see how the others were faring. Tracy's dad was wearing a suit and appeared to be almost as uncomfortable as I was. A couple of the others were using sheets of paper to fan themselves. Laura was sitting there as serene as can be; cool as a cucumber. I was jealous.

The principal finally stood up and addressed us. "It is the school's policy to suspend students in cases like this. The students involved were sent home on Friday and were not in class today. In order to suspend them for more than three days, they must be given a hearing in front of the school board. Hearings have been scheduled for tomorrow night. We plan to ask that they be suspended for a total of two weeks. In addition, they will be excluded from all extra-curricular activities for the rest of the school year. They will not be allowed to participate in sports, travel with the school band or act in school plays. They will be put on probation, and any further infractions will result in their being expelled. Your statements will be used against them, but the video won't be used unless they choose to fight the charges. We are quite sure that we can legally use the video, but unless it is necessary we don't want to pay for a legal opinion. You are entitled to attend the hearings, but are not required to be there. Does anybody have any questions?"

The extra-curricular stuff caught me by surprise. "Does that mean the school will need a new quarter-back and a new captain for the basketball team? Both of them were involved?" I asked.

"Yes. The swim team, wrestling team, jazz band and drama club will also lose members. We don't take this sort of behaviour lightly. We want to set a precedent to discourage others from doing the same thing. It's not your fault, it's theirs," said the principal.

It was hard to deny her logic. Besides it was nice of the principal to fill us in, but I knew that we no longer had any say in the proceedings. The school would act as the school saw fit.

No one else had a question for the principal. She thanked us for our time and apologized for the students' behaviour. I was impressed with this administrator and to my surprise I told her so. My feelings were echoed by the six Torino family members in the room. Those of us who weren't already standing stood up to leave. The guidance counsellor who had said nothing all afternoon suddenly jumped up and pointed to Tracy.

"Young lady, please hang on just a minute." We all stopped.

"I have been responsible for the video room and its monitors long enough. If you know so much about recording and electronic equipment, it will be a breeze for you to take it over. I'll see that you get the necessary time off from class. If you're as good as I think you are I will see that you get extra credit for doing all the school's filming."

Tracy was stunned; stunned in a very good way; too stunned to speak. Tracy too stunned to speak. It didn't happen often, but here it was. She could nod and stutter, but she could not speak!

The principal chuckled and looked to the guidance counsellor. "I think she said yes. That's got to be the shortest eviction in history. Half an hour ago she was banned from the room entirely, now she's expected to spend a good part of each day in it."

Turning to Tracy, she said, "I agree with her. I think you'll do a remarkable job. Have fun."

The school was empty by the time we were finished. I was going to be late getting to the wrecker's again. Laura saw me checking the clock. "Malcolm needs a ride to work. Let's move it. Chop! Chop!"

Her parents were as surprised at the outburst as I was, but they hustled out the door and insisted that giving me a ride was no problem what so ever.

I spent a couple of hours at the auto wrecker's. Laura was working at the theatre that night so I wouldn't see her. Instead, I got my uncle to drive me to the grocery store so I could shop. By the time I had everything on my list, my father's money was, indeed, gone. All gone, but for the eight dollars I spent on a can of wax for the Monte Carlo.

CHAPTER TEN

The rest of the week was interesting. There was nowhere near as much excitement as in the previous week, but it was interesting just the same. I still had not heard from my father, so I made another round of phone calls.

The results were the same. No one had heard from or seen him. This time I believed they were telling me the truth. Some of them sounded as worried as I felt. My father's disappearance was proving to be a problem, not just for me, but for others as well. If I wanted further proof of their concern, I received it one evening when the phone rang not once but twice. Only one number showed up on my call display. It was a well-known local lawyer and he asked me a number of questions regarding my father. I could tell from his questions that he did not have my or my father's best interests at heart. He was digging for information in an effort to protect someone. It had to be someone important, or at the very least someone who had access to large amounts of money. This lawyer did not come cheap. He left a number and told me to call if I heard anything. To my, almost sixteen-year-old ears, it sounded like he was threatening me.

The next call came within a few minutes of the first. The caller's identity was blocked. This time a two-year-old would have recognized the threat. If I knew anything about my father's plans, I was to keep quiet. If he told me the names of any of his friends, I was to keep them to myself. If I spoke out of turn to anyone, I would be hurt. I had no idea who was behind either call. I might have been able to figure it out but I really didn't care. I knew nothing about my father's business and wouldn't have told anyone if I did. If this was the kind of people you met living a life of crime, I would stay on the straight and narrow, Thank you, very much!

Tuesday was a quiet day in school. Most of the students were aware of the upcoming hearings. They must have been waiting for the results of the hearing because nothing was said to us until Wednesday. The Torino's and I opted not to attend the hearings. The school superintendent called Terry with the results. He told the rest of us.

A total of eight students were suspended. Five of them were involved in both incidents and three were only involved in one or the other. The two who were a part of the cookie crushing/hair cutting incident were given only a one week suspension. The rest were given two. The culprits all decided to accept their punishment, not because the video was powerful evidence against them, but because the moment the first accusation was made they all started ratting on each other.

The news spread quickly. The suspended students were all popular. They had a lot of friends and even more followers. The athletes, especially, had tons of adoring fans. We had no idea just how many there were until we had to face them. Despite our, and the principal's, best efforts to keep our names a secret, it was soon obvious that someone talked. I was betting on the vice-principal but it could have been any one of them.

The nearer Laura, Tracy and I got to the school on Wednesday morning, the louder the jeers grew. We were sworn at, called traitors, our ancestry was called into question and we were compared to history's worst villains. I was used to this kind of abuse, but I felt sorry for the girls. The taunts bothered Laura because I felt her grip on my hand tighten whenever someone made a particularly hurtful comment. I looked Tracy's way and saw her ever-present smile was still in place. I knew her well enough by now, however, to realize that it was a forced smile. We soldiered on. We walked with our backs straight and our heads held high. We refused to walk around our tormentors. Instead, we pointed ourselves straight at them and forced them to move out of our way.

We were met that morning by a group of students who were loud, brave and in your face. We could handle them. We were to learn that there was another group of students in the school and before the day was out we would meet a few of them. These students weren't loud or brave. They were simply scared – too afraid to meet us in public. I was approached in a washroom. A young man wanted to thank me but not here. I agreed to meet him in a park after school. I told Laura and Tracy about the incident so when someone pulled Laura into an out-of-the-way doorway with the same thing in mind, she asked them to join us. Tracy was picking up some lab equipment from a storage closet when someone whispered to her. Six of us met in the park.

Why were they scared? They were all victims of the same bunch of bullies who attacked us. They were either assaulted, had money stolen or were harassed. The bullies didn't need money. They didn't have to prove their strength. They only acted out because they thought it was fun to humiliate and hurt others. Until our meeting in the park, all three of our new friends thought they were the only victims. After our meeting, none of us would have been surprised to learn there were many others.

It was sheer coincidence that brought us together. No, it wasn't coincidence but thankfulness. The three people in front of us wanted to say thank you. They heard the rumours, and instead of resenting us, they wanted to show their appreciation for what we did. It was unfortunate that they had to approach us on the sly.

We tried to brush aside their gratitude but they were adamant. "If you want to thank someone, thank Tracy," I said. "She was the only one smart enough to carry recording equipment and the only one capable of using it. If not for her, instead of standing here, all of us would be hiding in a corner waiting for the next shoe to drop."

Laura saw what I was up to and jumped on the bandwagon. "She's a hero. They were yelling and threatening and Tracy was as calm as could be. She recorded everything they said and did."

Tracy's face was so red I thought a blood vessel might break. She tried to deny everything we said but the more she denied it, the more we poured it on. The looks of adoration she received from our new friends would have warmed the heart of the meanest Grinch. Instead of being the person who looked up to others, Tracy was now being looked up to. Just as the guidance counsellor knew she was capable of handling the video monitors, we knew she was capable of handling her new responsibilities as a leader.

Was our decision not to press charges, the right one? We were no longer sure. We talked about it with the others. We gave them Officer Joe Grosjean's name and phone number. We encouraged them to give him a call. It would be good for him to have their information, even if he didn't use it.

Thursday was a new day and new dynamics were at work. I arrived at school and was met by a small group of basketball players. Their leader stepped forward to face me. Before a word could leave his mouth, another young man ran up and grabbed him roughly by the arm. I didn't hear the conversation, but it was long and heated. It happened one more time while I was walking between classes. A student I didn't recognize grabbed my arm. Before he could spin me around one of his friends pushed him to the floor. It was odd behaviour and the only explanation I could come up with involved Joe. He must have made good on his promise to talk to our assailants. They took his threats seriously and now were trying to protect themselves by seeing that no harm came to us. Thanks Joe.

After work on Thursday, I met up with Scott Morgan. I told him what was happening in my life and he filled me in on his progress with the newsstand. I drank a diet cola - hated the stuff, but I had to watch my waist-line now that there was a girl in my life - while he drank coffee. Maybe it was weird to see a twenty-year-old socializing with a sixteen-year-old, but I enjoyed listening to his stories. His outlook on life was the total opposite of the Webb outlook. I liked his better.

It was Scott who told me about the tires that were stolen from the local tire manufacturer's compound. I tried to act nonchalant, but in reality my heart was racing. Could this be the big job my father was planning? Was a truck load of tires worth enough to retire? I wanted answers to these questions and several more, but was it safe for me to ask Scott or would he suspect that I had reasons other than curiosity for asking. I decided not to take a chance.

Instead, I waited until Scott was out the door of the restaurant. Once he climbed into the Firebird, I plugged several quarters into the newspaper vending machine and bought myself a paper. The news didn't make the front page but it held a prominent position on page two. A semi-trailer load of tires was stolen. They took the trailer and all. Someone with their own tractor backed up, hooked onto the trailer and drove away. According to the reporter, the load of tires had a wholesale value of between thirty-five and forty thousand dollars. The trailer was all, but worthless. No one would be able to register it for use on the highway. It was worth a few hundred dollars as a storage unit and the tires, if they were new, were worth a few hundred more. On the street, the load probably wasn't worth much more than fifteen thousand dollars. It was a lot of money, but it certainly wouldn't last someone a lifetime.

It might have been my father. I knew from past experience that it was something he could and would do. I thought back to what I learned from my uncle. Some of it fit, but not all of it. How did my uncle put it? It was to be a big score, the biggest ever and his last one. Fifteen thousand dollars wasn't nearly big enough. It wasn't my father. I was convinced.

It was dark when I rounded the corner near my home. To my dismay, I saw a police cruiser parked in front of the house. As I approached, I heard a horn honk and then I saw Dan Carruthers hurrying out of our backyard. He was out of breath, and at first, I thought he appeared to be in a state of panic. If it was panic, it didn't last long. "Where is your no-account father? I've been looking for him. Got any tires for sale? Just you wait. I've got your number. You'll get yours and very soon."

Before I had a chance to say a word, he jumped into the police cruiser with his partner and they peeled away from the curb. Before unlocking the front door, I checked the garage and the back yard. The windows and doors were fine. The Monte Carlo gleamed, its tires shone. I went inside the house.

My father had been here. On the counter was a wad of cash. I counted it. There was enough to pay the accumulated bills and a few dollars more. There was no note. I searched everywhere but found nothing. I looked at the money on the counter. I guess maybe my father was responsible for stealing the tires. He was lucky he wasn't here when Dan was snooping around. Why was Dan snooping around? How did he catch on to my father so soon? How did my father manage to sell the tires so quickly? The money must have come from the sale of the tires, didn't it? Should I spend the money? It was tainted, wasn't it? Questions, so many questions! It was enough to make my head spin.

By the time I woke up on Friday morning, I could only answer one of them. If I didn't use the money, the bills couldn't be paid. As uncomfortable as I felt about spending the money that was more than likely the proceeds of crime, I decided the bills just had to be paid.

I turned on the radio and dialled in a local news station. I wanted to find out if there was anything new on the tire theft. An announcement that a group of aliens from Venus were found rolling the tires into the Grand Canyon would have been nice. Instead I heard the announcer say there was nothing new to report. The culprits had made good their escape.

I listened to the rest of the newscast with a half an ear. "When we return from our commercial break, I'll give you the latest on the Tom Crawford story." The announcer had my attention.

The advertisements took an eternity. Cough drops; toilet bowl cleaner; Jeeps; insurance; if you want to buy it, this is where to go. Finally, the announcer returned.

"The body found in the burned out home last week was positively identified as Tom Crawford. Officials always suspected it was his body, but late yesterday afternoon they received the results of DNA tests. The tests prove beyond a reasonable doubt that it was Mr. Crawford. There is also a bit of a human interest angle to this story. A source at the city morgue tells us that they have been after the sole remaining relative of Mr. Crawford - his brother George - to make funeral arrangements. George Crawford refused. According to our source, he told officials that the city can pay for it. It seems that there was some bad blood between the brothers. Two years ago Tom collected a hundred-dollar reward by accusing his brother of painting graffiti on a park bench. George has not forgiven him. For now, the body remains in the morgue while the two sides argue. We will keep you posted on the outcome."

I guess I was wrong about the man I saw fleeing. It seems to me I was wrong a lot these days. Had I not almost convinced myself that my father was innocent of the tire theft? Oh well, I had to get to school. I had a Science test to write. Hopefully I would be right at least half of the time on that one.

One week until D-Day – D as in driver's license.

CHAPTER ELEVEN

The weekend passed quickly. I worked at the auto wrecker's all day Saturday. I went home, spent a good twenty minutes trying to get the grease stains out of my hands and finger nails and then enjoyed a three minute shower. I spent the evening with Laura at the movie theatre.

Thanks to my scrubbing efforts, I was allowed behind the concession stand. I became the soda fountain guy. Large Coke; medium Sprite; small Root Beer; I handled it all. After a couple of mishaps where I overfilled the cups, I learned exactly when to let go of the handle. I even learned that if I held the cup at just the right angle I could reduce the amount of foam. Wasn't I a genius?

The movie wasn't great. It involved a couple of bridges collapsing and the frantic efforts to save survivors. The end was typical. The hero saved the day, and of course he got the girl. The only thing unique about this movie - the hero was a mongrel dog, and the girl that he rode into the sunset with was a French Poodle.

After we finished cleaning up, we all jumped into the family van. Terry offered me a few dollars for helping out. I refused to take his money, so instead he drove us to a popular pizza restaurant and dropped us off. Laura was given more than enough money to pay for the pizza and pop.

I had spent a fair amount of time with Laura during the past couple of weeks, but this was the first time that it was just the two of us. Always before there were others with us, be it students or teachers at school, or Tracy or other Torino family members at home. It was the moment that I was both looking forward to, and dreading. I was looking forward to it, because who in his right mind would not want to be alone with a girl, especially a girl like Laura? I dreaded it, because I wasn't sure if we would have anything to talk about. I needn't have worried. We had lots to say to each other. An hour and a half passed. The pizza was gone, our soda glasses emptied for the second time – the waiter needed someone to show him what angle to hold the glass at to minimize the foam – and I still had thousands of questions for Laura. Her past; her future; I was curious about it all. By no means, was it a one-sided conversation. Laura now knew things about me that I don't think my parents ever knew and there were still thousands of things I wanted to tell her. I guess you can say that we found it easy to talk to one another, especially when we were by ourselves.

All too soon, it was time to call it a day. I walked Laura home and after taking a few minutes to say goodnight to her family, I headed for home. They would have given me a ride. In fact, they were a little upset that I had refused, but I wanted to walk. It wasn't that far and the exercise would do me good. Nothing was new at home.

I slept in on Sunday morning. Scott called about eleven-thirty and asked if I was available to help him set up his newsstand. It sounded like fun – who am I kidding, it sounded like work – but I agreed. The mall wasn't yet open when he picked me up so he insisted on buying lunch. We enjoyed a couple of fast-food burgers and went to work. His father arrived with a U-haul full of supplies. We spent the next four hours setting up displays and building shelves. The units were all designed so they could be closed and locked. If for some reason, Scott or whoever was working had to leave, they could simply lock everything up and go.

Later that afternoon, I was to meet Laura and Tracy. I phoned to say that I might be late. Wouldn't you know it the two girls showed up at the mall and happily went to work filling the shelves as we built them? It was a lot of work for those of us who were healthy and owned two good feet. You could see it was wearing on Scott, but he refused to give up. The closer we were to finishing and the sorer his leg grew, the more excited he was. Maybe it wasn't a dream job, but it represented some independence. In his shoes, I would have been just as happy. I might have been sitting and watching those without a disability do the work, but I would be happy.

While the others finished cleaning up, I dug my grocery list out of my pocket and headed to the grocery store. If anything, the list was longer than the week earlier. How could one person go through so much food? I had to dip into my own funds to come up with enough money to pay for my selections. Where was my father anyway?

Scott dropped Tracy, Laura and I off at my place. We spent the rest of the afternoon listening to music and polishing the Monte Carlo. I started the barbecue and cooked up a few wieners. Maybe it wasn't gourmet food, but we enjoyed it. Tracy noticed a blue truck parked down the street.

"That truck looks familiar", she said. "Where have I seen it before?"

Nobody could give her an answer and because the truck appeared to be empty, we forgot about it again.

On Monday, I stopped at the Drivers Licence office to make an appointment for that Thursday, the day of my birthday, to write my test. Because my jurisdiction was one of the few that didn't have a graduated licensing system, if I passed the written test, I could take the road test on Friday. I picked up the paperwork that I needed while I was there. A quick glance at the papers told me that I needed a parent or guardian's signature in three places. Where was my Father? I was starting to sound like a broken record.

That evening I called my mother. Without getting into detail, I told her that Dad was away and could she sign the papers if I sent them to her. She promised me she would. Time was growing short, so I opted to pay the extra money to send them by overnight express.

Nothing happened on Tuesday. I mean nothing at all. Things at school went well. For the first time that I could remember, no one was making remarks behind my back. Most of the suspended students still were not in class, so it must have been their friends that spread the word. Leave Webb alone.

Tracy was kept busy with her new duties. Almost overnight, she became one of the most popular girls in school. Tracy could make or break almost anyone. To film or not to film, it was up to Tracy. She could make you a star in your schoolmates' eyes, or she could make you look like a fool just by deciding when to turn on the cameras. Don't forget about the people from the park. Tracy was their hero. They would do anything for her and would do almost nothing without her approval. Tracy took it in stride. She made a lot of students look like stars and almost no one look the fool. Her advice to her hangers-on was always good advice. Laura was still her favourite and every morning she walked to school with us. She also left with us on the afternoons she wasn't filming some sporting event or another.

Laura was still Laura. Maybe she wasn't quite as shy, but she still avoided the lime - light. She didn't go out of her way to avoid the other girls, but she didn't encourage them to approach her either. As for the boys in our class - the further they stayed away from her, the better I liked it.

Before I could leave for school on Wednesday, the doorbell rang. I took a look out the window before opening the door. I half-expected to see Dan standing there, but to my relief I saw a courier's truck parked out front. I ran to the door. My mother came through. I had everything I needed to get my licence. Now all that was left was passing the test.

That afternoon I went to work at the wrecker's. I walked in the front door and said hello to a couple of my co-workers. Instead of giving me their usual flippant remarks, they turned away from me. Oh! Oh! What did I do wrong now? I didn't have to wait long to find out what was happening.

My uncle threw a copy of the day's paper onto the desk in front of me. The front page headline read: "Plot to steal shipment of pharmaceuticals foiled. Local thug is on the run!"

I looked from the paper in front of me to my uncle. "Read it all," he said.

The more I read, the more panicky I felt:

Police with the help of the pharmaceutical company's own security staff have foiled an attempt to steal a load of drugs worth millions of dollars. An informant has come forward with some details of the plan. The police and Security Staff investigated and found that most of what the informant said was true. Many of the details are being kept quiet, but we believe that the thieves were planning to steal the shipment of drugs once they were loaded on the truck for distribution. If you remember, we reported a theft last week that was very similar to the one planned here. A local tire manufacturer had a load of tires stolen. The police believe that last week's theft may have been a trial run.

A local man has been connected to the plot. Blake Webb, a forty-two year old resident of Parkfield, has been charged but never convicted of several crimes. The police have found a number of items they believe were going to be used in the commission of the theft. Fingerprints and other identifying marks on these tools lead the police to believe they belong to the forty-two year old Webb. The police are asking for the public's help in locating Blake Webb. He is five feet ten inches tall, weighs about one hundred and eighty pounds, has dark curly hair and sometimes wears a moustache. Our source in the police department tells us that Webb has more than likely fled the area. We remind our readers that Blake Webb must be considered innocent until he has been found guilty of this or any other crime.

Unless there was another Blake Webb that I never heard of, the man they were talking about was my father. "I don't suppose you have a cousin from another city named Blake," I asked my uncle.

"Afraid not," he said. "Your father is the only one I know. He's the only one the cops are looking for too. They've been here twice already. I drove by your house a while ago. They've been there. I'll give you a hand cleaning up. They left a mess."

He saw my look of panic and said, "I don't think they touched the Monte Carlo, but they broke the garage door trying to get in."

Finding car parts was the last thing on my mind, so my uncle drove me home. We were met by the police. I was thrown roughly into the back seat of a cruiser for the second time in my short life. My uncle was protesting. People two blocks over probably heard him protesting, but the cops ignored him. Two cops I didn't know began firing questions at me. Where is your father? When are you expecting him? Did you see him today? I could hear my uncle yelling at me to keep quiet.

"I'll call you a lawyer. Don't say anything until he gets here. Malcolm's a minor. You can't question him without an adult present." My uncle was persistent, but so were the police. They kept firing their questions at me. I sat in the seat and said nothing.

I remained silent even as I saw Dan Carruthers walk out of my house carrying my computer. His partner followed with a folder full of papers that came from the drawer where my father kept his important documents. These items were thrown into a car and the two men returned to the house. On their way back to the house, they detoured across the neighbour's lawn, to the sprinkler that was running. Once their boots were good and wet, they walked across the flower garden in front of our house. They looked my way and laughed as they entered the house with mud-caked boots.

Their fun lasted another twenty minutes. It only took twenty minutes for the lawyer, my uncle called, to arrive. Not many lawyers would drop everything to drive to a client's home, but this one did. The Webb's were some of his steadiest customers. The lawyer was irate when he saw what was happening. There must have been some weight to at least some of his threats, because all of a sudden I was let out of the car, and at least six officers came out of the house. The last one out made a half-hearted attempt to close the shattered door. After three attempts, he decided it was futile, gave the lawyer a sheepish grin and joined his partner in the street.

The house was a shambles. There was mud from one end to another. The drawers were pulled out and dumped on the floor. The contents of the closets were scattered everywhere. The beds were turned upside down. The computer, answering machine and several flash drives that I kept in a desk were missing. One of the flash drives contained an essay that I was working on for school. The essay was due in a few days so the lawyer told me he would do what he could to get it back. The aforementioned papers were missing. The place was such a mess that I would probably never know what else was gone.

The phone started ringing almost immediately. First, it was Laura who called. "I heard about your father. Are you okay? I'm coming over." Before I could reply, she hung up and ten minutes later her mother dropped her off in front of the house. Thank heavens; the police were gone before they arrived.

The next call was from my mother. One of her old friends had called her to pass on the news. I told her what was happening. There was no use trying to hide anything now. Her reply, "I'll be there sometime tomorrow. I'm catching the first flight out." It would be good to see her.

My uncle made a couple of calls and Laura made a couple of calls. Soon I had a houseful of Torino's, working side by side, with some of our town's seedier characters. The only thing they had in common was a desire to cheer me up while they cleaned up the mess left behind by the police. It was fun to listen to their joking and teasing. A lot more fun than watching the police tear your home apart anyway.

Once the house was presentable again, a collection was taken and pizzas were ordered. Tracy found the movie "Twister" in a box and to everyone's delight she put it in the DVD player. The pizza arrived and a lengthy argument about what did the most damage ensued. The law abiding Torino's felt a twister was worse than the cops. My uncle's friends insisted the cops could do the most damage. By the time the movie climaxed with the mother of all tornados, everyone was in agreement. Mother Nature won.

CHAPTER TWELVE

Finally, Thursday was here. I wish I could say I slept like a baby and would have slept until noon, if the alarm hadn't woken me up. That just didn't happen. I tossed and turned all night. I gave up on sleep long before the alarm sounded. I tried to chase the not-so-nice thoughts - my father's troubles and my own undeserved problems with the police - with nice thoughts: getting my driver's licence, the Monte Carlo and new friends. It didn't work. All my imagination would let me see was police, courthouses and jail cells.

At school, no one would come near me. Even the teachers acted as though I was carrying the Bubonic Plague and avoided me. Laura and Tracy were with me, of course. I suggested that they might want to keep their distance for a few days just in case my bad vibes were contagious. Their response: they each grabbed one of my arms and marched me down the center of the hallway.

The day dragged on. I left my last class a few minutes early, so I had enough time to make my appointment for the driver's test. Laura accompanied me downtown and sat patiently while I filled out all the required paperwork. She would be going through the same routine in six weeks or so. I hoped I would be around to return the favour.

Finally, I was handed the test and sent to a quiet cubicle to complete it. Ten minutes later, I was finished. Was the test that easy, or did I do something drastically wrong? It took longer to get my mark than it took to write the test. I aced it! All those signs - I knew them all. Right turns, left turns, merging with traffic, stopping distances - they couldn't fool me. It was a proud young man who walked out of the office that afternoon with a driver's licence in one hand and a pretty girl in the other. Yes I was proud, but I was extremely worried as well.

It was too late to go to the auto wrecker's so Laura walked home with me. For the second day in a row, I wasn't going to make any money. That was going to have to stop. The registration and insurance for the Monte Carlo was going to cost me a small fortune. I was going to try and round up a licensed driver who could ride shotgun while I took the Monte Carlo on its maiden journey. I had Scott in mind, but when we arrived home, the door was open and my mother was busy puttering in the yard. We shared a long hug and to be honest, just a few tears. I introduced my two favourite ladies - sorry Tracy; I'll include you next time. "Laura, meet my mother, Veronica." They hit it off immediately. I was sure they would but the way my luck was running, I wouldn't have bet on it.

We entered the house and mom went to work making supper. The last time I sat at the kitchen table and watched my mother make supper was what, six or seven years ago? I felt like a little kid again. The feeling only lasted until she asked me to spill it. "What's been happening? Why haven't I been informed?" she wanted to know.

I started from the beginning and told her everything that had happened since the fire. I told her why I had kept her in the dark. I honestly thought that dad would be home any time. The money on the counter was proof he was keeping in touch wasn't it?

It was a good point. I told her all about yesterday's events; the police, the mess they made, my uncle's friends and the Torino family all helping to clean up. I told her about the lawyer and gave her his phone number. I sat in the kitchen enjoying the smells of cooking biscuits, pork chops and hash browns – all my favourites – while she went to the other room and called the lawyer to make an appointment.

She returned to the kitchen just in time to take the golden-brown biscuits from the oven. "We have an appointment for Saturday morning. He tells me there is some issue with a flash drive and essay. He hopes to have it for you then. If necessary, he knows a judge who will compel them to hand it over. Eat Up! Don't you want to take your car for a test drive?"

We left the dishes in the sink and went outside. I opened the garage door and carefully backed the Monte Carlo out far enough for the others to get in without straining themselves. With a dramatic gesture, my mother fastened her seat belt. "Is this contraption safe," she asked? "Do you think you can drive it? Maybe you should let me take the wheel."

She was joking of course. She trusted me, I think.

Following my mother's directions I drove to a large parking lot and proved to her that I could manoeuvre the car. She even made me practice parallel parking. It was easy to park the car. A lot easier than parking the grain truck was, anyway. When we left the parking lot, she asked me to make a series of right and left hand turns. If I made any mistakes, she didn't tell me about them. When she was sure, I could drive on the city streets, she directed me to the highway. For the very first time, I had the opportunity to feel the Monte Carlo's power. I was careful not to speed, but that feeling of power was all I dreamt it would be.

All too soon, it was time to head back towards the city. I was going to make the turn that led to our house, but mom insisted I take the next turn-off. Before I knew, it we were at my grandparents. Their normally quiet street was filled with vehicles. The only parking spot available was right in front of the house. The spot wasn't any more than big enough to fit the Monte Carlo in, but I tried it anyway. I was so busy watching what I was doing that I didn't notice the huge crowd gathering in the yard. When at last I had the car parked precisely where it belonged, to my surprise, I received a standing ovation.

I climbed out of the car to a chorus of happy birthdays.

"Surprised?" my mother asked.

Tracy was there with Laura's brother, Bob. Most of the guys from work were there, and of course, all the Webb's. Everybody was there but my father. It was a great time, none the less. There was a huge birthday cake and a couple of pails of ice cream. I received a number of gifts. A sweater, some socks from one of my aunts, several gift certificates for car washes and my co-workers gave me a couple of the tools that they knew I wanted. Before I knew it, it was time to leave. The same crowd gathered on the lawn and cheered when I managed to get the Monte Carlo back on the street.

I parked the car in the garage. I grabbed a cloth and wiped off some of the road grime. Before I closed the door, I took one last look. The years of hard work, the money I spent, the waiting; it was worth it all.

On Friday morning, I walked to school for what I hoped was the last time. The school day was much the same as the day before. I may as well have been hiding in a closet for all the attention I was getting. I was behind in my homework and I was a little worried that I might be called upon in class to give an answer that I didn't know. I worried for nothing. The teachers continued to ignore me.

My mother picked me up that afternoon in the Monte Carlo so I could take the road test. Laura had a few things to pick up for her mother after school so she wasn't with me. My examiner was a sour-faced old battle-axe who wouldn't have cracked a smile at the sight of a new born baby or a cute little fluffy white kitten. She sounded a lot like a drill instructor as she began issuing orders. I thought I was blowing it. She would give me an instruction, and out of the corner of my eye I could see her shaking her head and the tsks, tsks were clearly audible. Another instruction, another head shake and she gave me another tsk tsk. When at last I pulled into the designated parking spot in front of her office, I expected the worst. Instead I was handed a report that showed only two minor mistakes. I ran inside with it and twenty minutes later, I came out with a full-fledged driver's licence.

I dropped mom off at home and drove to work. You heard me, I drove! The first thing I did when I arrived was make a sign, "Reserved for Malcolm Webb." I took my sign to the parking spot furthest from the office and attached it to the fence. Now there were two reserved parking spots, one for the handicapped and one for me.

Nothing special happened while I was working. I removed an engine coolant reservoir from a wrecked Ford Fusion and with the help of one of the tow truck drivers; I removed the drive-shaft from a Chevrolet Blazer. I carried the items to the office so their new owners could pick them up the next day. By the time I was finished, it was too late to help Laura out at the movie theatre. I took the opportunity to go for a drive. I cranked up the music and spent the next half-hour driving around town.

The clock on the dash read eight forty-five. I wasn't expected anywhere, so I pulled into the mall parking lot and ran inside to see Scott. He was locking up his kiosk as I approached. I waved to him, making sure he saw the car keys dangling from my hand. He gave me one of his patented grins. "You passed your tests, congratulations," he said! "Any chance I can get a ride home? The Firebird died on me this morning."

Scott wanted a cup of coffee. For the first time, I found myself sitting behind the wheel while I waited at a drive-through. I couldn't help but wonder how many more times I would find myself doing the same thing in my lifetime. Hundreds - for sure, thousands - probably, a million - who knew? I ordered Scott a coffee and a soda for myself. Scott filled me in on his day while I drove. I took the long way so he would have lots of time. The newsstand was doing okay. Each day, his business was picking up. He managed to break-even last week and he was confident there was more to come. I dropped him off at home. He thanked me for the ride and I promised him I would try to locate a starter for the Firebird.

My mother was waiting for me when I got home. Having a son old enough to drive was something new to her, and I could see she was worried. To her credit, she kept the worry to herself. I threw in a load of laundry and sat down in the living room to talk with her. She brought up a subject I wanted to avoid in the worst way. What would happen to me if my father was arrested, found guilty and sent to jail? I could, of course, move in with her. She had talked to her new husband and he assured her that I was welcome. At this very moment, he was cleaning out a room. The thought made me shudder. They lived hundreds of miles away. The Webb's lived in Parkfield. I went to school in Parkfield. I had a job in Parkfield. My friends were in Parkfield. Yes, I can say friends - plural. Weren't both Tracy and Scott friends? What about Laura? For the first time in my life, I met someone who wanted to be with me and now I might have to move away. We agreed to wait a couple of days before making a final decision. Where was my father?

I phoned Laura. If you think it was a short call, think again. She told me about that night's movie. It was a slasher flick where several young people met their demise at the hands of a demented killer. I didn't regret missing it. Before hanging up - I could hear her parents in the background telling her to get off the phone - we made plans for the weekend. Before going to bed, I checked to make sure I locked the doors, including the garage door. I wasn't really surprised to see a police car parked on the street.

Later that evening the phone started ringing. Relatives called, my mother's friends called, my uncle called, Scott called and Laura called. Turn on the radio, turn on the TV, check the news and pick up a newspaper. My mother and I turned the TV to a local news station just in time to watch Dan Carruthers walk up to a bank of microphones.

The circumstances called for someone who was cool, calm, collected, serious and professional. Instead, the cameras were pointed at Dan. Too many donuts and too many nights sitting behind the wheel of a cruiser, made the dress uniform he was wearing too small. His hair was slicked back and he looked ridiculous. Okay, maybe I was being a little harsh but I didn't like the guy, so sue me.

Dan was clearly enjoying the limelight. He held up his arms in an effort to get the reporters around him to be quiet. A couple of them kept talking and it was all Dan could do to keep the smile on his face. His face grew redder and redder until someone in the crowd called for silence.

Dan referred to some written notes and began to speak. "The Parkfield police department has called this press conference to announce further charges against a local resident. You will remember that we announced on Wednesday that we were looking for Blake Webb. He is accused of being the mastermind behind the theft of a truckload of tires and the attempted theft of a truck-load of pharmaceuticals. Today, we are announcing that he is also charged with murdering Tom Crawford. Tom's body was found in his burned out house, a couple of weeks ago. I and other members of the force have spent innumerable hours investigating this crime. I am pleased to say that I have irrefutable proof that Blake Webb is guilty. I won't go into details at this time, but rest assured the moment Webb is located you will hear more. This city will not tolerate these sorts of crime and it will not tolerate these sorts of criminals. We will find Blake Webb. Anybody, friends or family, found to be helping Webb will be charged as accessories. If you, or someone you know, has information that will assist us in locating Blake Webb please call me, Dan Carruthers at the Parkfield Police Department.

Oh! Oh!

CHAPTER THIRTEEN

Another sleepless night! I climbed out of bed on Saturday morning long before the alarm went off. I wasn't the only one who couldn't sleep. The smell of frying bacon coming from the kitchen told me that my mother was also awake. Ordinarily the smell of bacon cooking reminded me of better times – long, lazy Saturdays with mom and dad talking quietly in the kitchen, making plans to visit family, or if I was really lucky getting ready to drive to the lake. Unfortunately, there was nothing ordinary about this Saturday morning.

The previous night's earth-shattering news made our planned visit to the lawyer twice as important. I washed, dried and put the breakfast dishes away while my mother showered and dressed. Once she finished in the bathroom, it was my turn. Fifteen minutes later I was ready to go. I looked at the digital clock on the stove. Our appointment was still two hours away.

I poured myself a glass of juice and my mother a cup of instant coffee. We sat across the kitchen table from one another. She told me that she was flying home the following day. She felt that once we talked to the lawyer, there was very little else she could accomplish here. She was expected at her job on Monday morning. She went on to tell me that she felt I would be safer with her. I could pack a few things this trip and maybe come spring break or summer vacation, I could return for the rest. The Monte Carlo would have to stay of course, but I would be allowed to use the family sedan on occasion.

Although she was my mother, I looked at her and saw a stranger. Not a stranger exactly. Strangers didn't know your favourite foods. Strangers didn't travel half-way across the country to make sure you were okay. I knew my mother loved me and I knew I loved my mother, but things were different between us. She had her life with her new family and I had my life here in Parkfield. Maybe the people in Parkfield weren't the friendliest. Maybe they weren't willing to forgive and forget, especially us Webb's but they were my people. Going away with my mother might solve my problems and it probably would be safer for me, but at that moment I knew it would be a mistake to leave. How was I going to convince the lady sitting across from me?

How could I abandon my father? Maybe, he needed my help. How could I be of any assistance if I wasn't right here where he could find me? Shouldn't I be out there trying to find him?

She countered my arguments. You're not abandoning him. If he needs your help, he knows you'll be with me. He has his family here to help him. What can a sixteen-year-old do to locate him?

What about school? What about my job? What about Laura?

She admitted that switching schools was a problem, but not an insurmountable problem. I could find a new job. There were thousands of auto wrecker's in the world. Maybe this would be a good opportunity to look for something else. There were supermarkets, gas stations, lawn-care companies and hundreds of other employers looking for help. As for Laura, she knew I would miss her, but had I not just met her. How attached could we possibly be after just a couple of weeks? I would find someone else. A fine upstanding young man like me could have my choice of dates.

I wasn't buying it, not for a minute but I was smart enough to know I was losing the argument. I was grasping for straws when I told her about Dan Carruthers insisting that I not leave the area. I told her that I was a Webb and Webb's don't run.

Before she could respond, there was a knock at the door. I moved the usual corner of the blind aside to see who it was. It was my uncle from the wrecker's and I had an idea. I told my mother I would be right back and went to let him in. By the time the two of us made it to the kitchen, we had reached an understanding.

I poured my uncle a cup of coffee and refilled my mother's cup. I was about to put the pot back on the burner when I decided that maybe drinking coffee would make me look more like an adult, so I poured the last cup for myself. I tried it black. It was horrible so I put a bit of sugar in it. It was still horrible so as a last resort, I added some milk just as my uncle had. This stuff wasn't bad at all; I think I could get used to this.

Uncle Sid has promised that he will move into the house with me until we hear from dad. He says he will pay the utilities – phone, cable, power and whatever. I'll keep working and will contribute where I can. Dad has left money twice now. Maybe, he will leave some more. We will make do until school is out. Once school is out, we can talk about it again if we haven't heard from him.

I was afraid to look my mother in the eye. I was afraid she would say no. Instead, she gave Uncle Sid a steely glance. "Do you promise to look out for him?" she asked. "He told me a moment ago he wanted to be like the Webb's who don't run and that's fine, but I need your promises that he won't be like the Webb's who are always breaking the law. I'll send a few dollars each month for groceries. This is just until school is out though."

My uncle gave his word that I would be looked after. He promised to move his things in later that day and he, himself would move in on Sunday, after my mother left for the airport. I gave a sigh of relief.

On the way to the lawyer's office, my mother asked, "What's the real reason you want to stay, the car or the girl?"

The question caught me by surprise and I almost drove off the road. I thought about it until we pulled into the complex that housed the lawyer's office. "Both," I said. "I don't want to leave either of them."

We were the only ones in the office. No secretaries, no file clerks and no other lawyers. I hardly recognized the man who opened the door for us. The last time I saw the lawyer, he was wearing a suit that probably cost as much as my car. Today, he was wearing an old pair of sweat pants and a tattered sweater. He apologized for his clothes, saying, "I just got back from walking the dog at the dog park."

He sat us down in an outer office and got down to business. "Who am I representing and who is going to pay me?" he wanted to know. This guy was good. He could turn it on or off at the drop of the hat. On Wednesday, he was my white knight protecting me from the big bad bullies that called themselves cops. Right now, it was me he was making feel like the villain. How dare I ask for his help without first offering money? His time was valuable. He had dogs to walk. Who cares about the poor and the downtrodden? Maybe I was wrong to feel put out, but that's how I felt.

He eased up a little bit and began to explain the situation. "I can represent young Malcolm here if you like, or I can represent Blake's interests. I can't represent both. I will need a retainer, either way. Malcolm may be able to receive financial assistance from the government. I'm not sure. That will depend on the family income. I personally don't check on these things, but I have staff that can do that. They can look into it on Monday, if you wish. In the meantime, I need a five-hundred dollar retainer and a signature; Blake's, if I am to represent him, or Malcolm's and a guardian, if that is who I am going to represent." He looked from my mother to me and back again.

This was a way over my head. I could tell by the look on her face that my mother was in over her head, as well. Twenty minutes later, we left the office. My mother was five-hundred dollars poorer, but I had a lawyer. We had no idea what he was going to do for me. We weren't even sure that I needed a lawyer. We entered his office thinking we would get answers to our questions. What is happening? What do we do? What can we expect? We left with even more questions. What a bummer!

I dropped my mother off at the house and drove to work. I love the sound of that. Can I say it again? I drove to work. It was quiet for a Saturday. That's probably a good thing because I spent a good part of the afternoon answering questions about my father. No, I did not know where he was. No, he did not kill anyone. Yes, I was sure about that.

On the other hand, maybe being quiet wasn't a good thing. Few customers meant even fewer tips. The point was driven home when the manager gave me my pay check. The check and tips combined didn't add up to much, but it was going to have to do.

I managed to find a starter for Scott's Firebird that was in good condition. I removed it from the donor car and after paying for it - less employee discount - I put it in the trunk. I was about to call it a day when a farmer came in, and asked for a water pump for his truck. It wasn't hard to find. The yard was full of old Chevrolet pick-ups. He helped me take it off and gave me five dollars for my troubles. Farmers, you've got to love them.

Mom promised to cook one last meal before she left the following morning. She invited Laura over and at my suggestion she included Tracy. I picked up Laura first. Her father insisted that I take him for a drive. He wanted proof that I knew what I was doing, before he allowed Laura to ride with me without an adult present. I guess I passed his test because he allowed me to leave with her. Two minutes later, I pulled up in Tracy's yard. I had to repeat the process with her father. I was getting tired of these drivers' tests. Maybe, it wasn't my driving. Maybe, they just wanted to ride in the Monte Carlo. Yes, that had to be it.

It was a beautiful evening, so we sat in the back yard while the chicken cooked on the barbecue. Mom made a pitcher of iced tea and another of lemonade. My mother was known for making excellent iced tea and lemonade. I had a hard time choosing between the two, so I drank a glass of each. For the most part, I sat back and listened as the girls got to know my mother a little better and vice versa. The chicken was cooked to perfection and went well with the salad and baked potatoes. A movie followed. Yes, it was a chick flick. I was outnumbered three to one wasn't I?

Once the movie was over, it was time to take the girls home. Laura and I dropped Tracy off and then joined Laura's parents in their kitchen for a cup of hot chocolate. It was nearly midnight when I left, but I still had things on my mind. I drove by the police station and thought of Joe Grosjean. I wondered if he could answer my questions. There was only one way to find out. I turned around and went back to the cop shop.

The officer manning the front desk was Dan Carruthers' partner. It could have been worse. Dan Carruthers, himself might have been there. This was something I hadn't taken into consideration. I noticed the name tag on his shirt pocket, "Ross Hanover," it read. Ross was anything but polite, when he asked me what I wanted. His language might have made the devil blush. I ignored his surly attitude and asked if Joe was available. He stood and stared at me for a good twenty seconds before he walked over to the radio and put out a call for Joe. Joe responded immediately, and when he learned there was somebody at the station to see him he promised to return a.s.a.p.

I wasn't offered a chair to sit on, so I decided to wait for Joe outside. He saw me standing there and pulled over to the curb. He opened the passenger door and told me to jump in. "We'd best talk someplace else," he said.

I got in and he drove around the block. It took but a moment to get the pleasantries out of the way. He noticed the Monte Carlo parked in the visitor's lot. "Nice car," he said. "Is it yours?"

I told him that it was and gave him a brief history on it. He asked how I was doing at school. I told him that things were better thanks to his intervention. He assured me that he was only doing his job. He asked if I changed my mind about pressing charges. I told him no. Pressing charges against school bullies was the furthest thing from my mind. He nodded at that.

Joe pulled into a parking lot where he could watch a group of young people who were gathered on the street. Without taking his eyes off the crowd, he asked, "Are you wondering about your father?"

I admitted I was. I told him about the trip to the lawyer and how disappointed I was in its outcome. "I'm afraid that I can't give you any good news. The autopsy shows that someone bashed Tom Crawford's skull in. Carruthers and his partner are sure that it was your father who did the bashing. They say that they have evidence. What that evidence is, I have no idea, but they must have something because the higher-ups in the department are behind them all the way."

"What about the man I saw leaving the fire?" I wanted to know. "It certainly wasn't my father. I would have recognized him, but it might have been the actual killer. Has anybody checked into that? Has anybody talked to the people in the neighbourhood to see if they saw anything?"

"I'm sorry to say, but the department refuses to believe there was anyone leaving that night. I brought it up and was quickly reminded that I was a patrolman not an investigator. I reminded them that Dan was also a patrolman and they were listening to his opinion. It was Dan who convinced them that you were lying, just to protect your father. They told me to mind my own business."

The group of kids broke up and Joe started the car and pulled out onto the street. He headed in the direction of the police station. "I'm sorry. If there is anything I can do to help I will, but in the meantime if you want to help your father, you must convince him to turn himself in."

He stopped behind the Monte Carlo and I got out. "I have one more question," I told him. "Why does Dan Carruthers keep turning up in this? Why has he made a mission of destroying my family?"

"That is the million dollar question," he said.

CHAPTER FOURTEEN

Looking at my watch, I discovered that it was very late by the time I finally got home. I decided to sneak into the house so as not to wake up my mother. Note to self-living alone might be lonely, but you don't have to sneak around.

I opened the door as quietly as its oil-less hinges allowed. Once I was inside, I listened for sounds and heard nothing. I knew the house like the back of my hand so turning on the light was a waste of time. I took one step and fell on my butt. I tripped over a pile of belongings that Uncle Sid had left sitting just inside the door. The noise would have wakened the dead so it was no surprise when my mother came running into the room waving an umbrella. The sight of her in her housecoat, her hair all tangled and waving that umbrella was hilarious. Forgetting all about my aches and pains from my fall, I burst out laughing. I must have been quite a sight lying in the middle of trash bags full of clothes and boxes of shoes because she burst out laughing too. Note to self-practice sneaking around.

The next morning, I filled a travel mug with coffee for my mother. Remembering that the stuff wasn't too bad with the right amount of cream and sugar, I dug out another travel mug and filled it for myself. It was a time for melancholy. Bringing her bags to the door, I loaded them into my car. We didn't have much to say to one another on the trip to the airport, but once her bags were checked she gave me a huge hug and said, "Promise me you will take care of yourself. Call if you need anything. There is a room for you with me. All you have to do is ask. Don't let your father drag you into trouble. I know he didn't kill that Crawford guy but if you try to hide him, take him food or otherwise help you might find yourself in as much trouble as he is. I almost forgot, drive slow and safe."

I returned the hug and answered, "I promise, yes, yes, yes, okay, I understand and yes, I'll drive safe."

I waited at the airport until her plane took off. Well, I waited until "a" plane took off. How was I to know if it was hers or not. It's not like I could see her waving from the window or anything like that.

My next stop was Scott's. I opened the Monte Carlo's trunk and took out his starter and a pair of coveralls. I tried wiggling my way underneath the Firebird to remove the old starter – fat chance, or should I say "fat me." I was going to have to jack it up and place blocks under it. No problem – it would just take a little longer. Two hours later, the Firebird was back on the ground, and when Scott turned the key it actually started. It still didn't run all that great, but at least it started. Scott paid me for the starter. I didn't charge him anything to install it so he invited me to stay for lunch. After I ate a bowl of soup and two roast beef sandwiches with mayonnaise, I knew I wouldn't fit under the Firebird any time in the near future.

Scott was going to look at apartments and I was supposed to pick up Laura and Tracy to drive to the lake. Tracy was waiting at Laura's when I pulled up. They jumped in the car almost before I came to a complete stop. They both carried small tote bags that I guessed carried swim suits and towels. Tracy also had her backpack with her. If anything the bag looked to be getting bulkier and heavier every day.

On the way to the lake, we made a slight detour and stopped at their grandfather's farm to say hello. He came out of the house when we drove up. "I see you passed your test," he said. "That is a nice car. You've put some work into it."

The blush and smile these compliments elicited from me were automatic. What could I say? I thanked him and made a point of telling him that his help made the test a whole lot easier. The girls went into the house to say hello to their grandmother. Ten minutes later, they were back with a box full of pastries, preserves and homemade juice. Everything we needed for a picnic at the beach. We drove out of the yard. I took a look out the rear view mirror and saw the elder Torino's standing in the doorway waving.

It was a hot sunny day. It was Sunday. Guess what! The beach was packed.

Finding a parking spot was tough. Finding enough room on the beach to spread out a blanket was even tougher. We wound up parking a good half mile away from the beach and spreading our blanket on a patch of course grass around a corner and out of sight of the main beach. We unpacked our supplies and the girls went off to change into swim suits. While I was waiting for them to return, I went for a walk along the shore. I was hoping to find a patch of flowers, something I could give to Laura and Tracy to put in their hair. It didn't look promising. There was no sand beach here. There was the small patch of grass next to the water where we spread our blanket, but the rest was all rocks. I was climbing on one such rock; it must have been a good six feet above the water level, when something struck me on the head and I fell.

The next thing I remembered I was being dragged through the water. I opened my eyes and saw a very worried-looking Laura trying to pull me to shore with Tracy's help. "Thank heavens," she said when she saw my eyes open. "I thought you were dead. Are you okay? You have blood on your head. You could have drowned. What happened?"

It took me a moment to answer. Even if I wasn't still a little groggy, seeing Laura in that swim suit left me breathless. When at last I gathered my wits, I pointed to the rocks. "I was climbing over there and something hit me." I noticed a large branch floating in the water. It had to be at least four feet long and was easily as big around as my arm. "Maybe it was that branch over there. Did it get blown down as I walked past? I didn't notice it floating before."

I was already wet, so I waded back into the water. Tracy threw me a towel so I dipped it into the water and wiped the blood from my head. When I was sure it was all wiped off, I dunked my head under water a time or two to try and clear the cobwebs. It seemed to work. I felt better but I was going to have at least two bumps. One was already the size of an egg and it was still growing, the other was smaller, but was just as painful. I wouldn't be wearing a hat for a couple of days.

I made my way to the branch and carried it to shore. I checked the butt end. It wasn't a fresh break. I looked toward the trees that were growing closest to the shore. If this branch was blown by the wind, it must have been quite a gust. The nearest tree was twenty feet away. There hadn't been a breath of wind all day. This was not an accident.

I threw modesty to the wind and walked behind the nearest tree to remove my wet clothes. I put on my trunks and spread my shirt and pants out to dry. I sat on the blanket and Tracy and Laura immediately began fussing over me. I thought back to my earlier actions. The small bump on my head was the result of something hitting me, probably the branch. I wasn't sure how I got the larger bump, but I guessed I hit my head on a rock when I fell. I might have been unconscious but I don't think I was out for very long. I was already feeling a lot better. Should I or should I not mention that fact to the girls? I enjoyed their attentions for a few more minutes until my conscience got the better of me.

I told them of my concern that I was hit intentionally. Tracy reached for the backpack and started pulling things out. First, it was the camera. She took pictures of the bruises on my head. She took pictures of the branch that now sat on shore and she took pictures of the rocks where I fell. With our help, she climbed up on the rocks and looked around. She noticed something on the ground. The camera whirred. She pointed to an area where something had laid half buried until recently. "I think I found the spot where that branch was laying. See behind that rock. Someone was kneeling. You can see where his toes and knees dug in." The camera whirred some more. "I'll take impressions in a moment." Then she said, "Mel! You'd better see this."

The only other person who called me Mel was my grandmother. It sounded a lot better coming from Tracy. I climbed up beside her. There it was plain as day; plain as the nose on your face; sticking out like a sore thumb, a boot print. Not just any boot print, this boot had a crack all the way across the sole. Tracy took her impressions. After taking a dip in the lake and eating some of the dainties, we decided it was time to head back to the city. Instead of taking the well-traveled path back to the parking lot, Tracy headed off into the trees where she found another trail. Twice she stopped to take pictures of the now-familiar boot print. We followed the prints to the parking lot where they disappeared near a set of tire tracks. Tracy's camera whirred once more and while I went to get the Monte Carlo, she took impressions of the tire tracks.

The main topic of discussion on the long ride into town was my safety. Was someone trying to hurt me? I suddenly remembered the blue truck that nearly ran me over. Was that an accident or was someone trying to hurt me that night too? Suddenly I wasn't sure. If someone was trying to hurt me, or God forbid, trying to kill me, why? Did I know something? Was I a threat to someone? Most important of all, if I was in danger were the girls safe traveling with me?

I mentioned my worries to Laura and Tracy which they brushed aside. Laura said, "You're the only one who has been attacked. They couldn't care less about us. The only one who needs protection is you. So, how do we protect you? Go to the police. You talked to them last night and they think you're lying, so we have to prove you're not lying. We know that there was someone in the alley. We know that the same person was at the lake. We should talk to the people who live near the fire, maybe they saw him too. Maybe we can figure out who it is. What do you say? Do we talk to them tonight?"

We parked the car at the end of the street and checked things over. We decided that there were only ten houses that had the same view of the alley as I did that night. I knocked on the first door. Someone looked out the window at me and the lights in the entire house went out. I knocked, rang the bell and knocked again. Nobody answered the door. I went to the next house. The door was opened immediately and a middle-aged lady I didn't recognize said, "You're that Webb kid. Beat it before I call the cops."

This wasn't working. No one would talk to me, the son of a murderer. Tracy offered to try her luck. I was doubtful. I didn't think anyone would take her seriously. She was only fourteen, and in many ways looked it. I carefully explained this to her, hoping not to hurt her feelings.

In her lifetime, Laura had watched hundreds of movies and thousands of actresses plying their trade so what happened next shouldn't have come as a surprise. Laura reached for her purse. A little lipstick here, a touch of eye shadow there, the jacket my mother forgot to take with her, a flick of her long dark hair, a slight straightening of her shoulders and what a few seconds ago was a young teenager, was now a young woman of the world brimming with confidence and charm. Laura looked as good as any news anchor in town. "Watch this," she said, and off she went. All Tracy and I could do was look on in astonishment. An hour later, she had visited with everyone who was home. A total of eight houses were scratched from our list. No one had seen anyone in the alley, but they all saw that no-good Webb kid thrown in the police cruiser. Our evening's endeavours were a complete bust.

We sat in the car wondering what we could do next. Until the people on our list returned home, there wasn't much that we could do. It was time for me to take the girls home. We stopped at Tracy's first. Laura and I went inside with her and waited while she brought out the impressions she made shortly after the fire and we compared them to the ones she made today. The footprints matched perfectly just as we knew they would, but we were surprised to see that today's tire tracks were also a match to those taken earlier.

The last stop was at Laura's. Okay, Okay! Maybe, we did spent a little too much time in the car before Laura went inside, but we didn't do anything indecent.

The lights were all on when I arrived home. At first, I thought my father must be home, but then I remembered Uncle Sid was moving in today. He was watching TV. I asked if I might join him for a while. I had homework to do, but like most guys my age I wasn't looking forward to doing it.

My uncle made room on the couch and I sat down grabbing a handful of chips from the bowl that he had sitting next to him. He asked me about my day. I told him about falling, but I didn't tell him why. He examined the bumps that were now a bright purple. He asked me a series of questions designed to determine if I still had my wits about me. I must have answered correctly because he abruptly sat down again and said, "You'll live. Good thing you hit your head and not your big toe. You might have hurt yourself if you hit your toe."

I pretended to take a swing at him. He ducked. I wandered off to my room and the homework that was waiting for me.

CHAPTER FIFTEEN

Monday morning arrived all too soon. My uncle walked into the kitchen as I was pouring coffee. No, I wasn't addicted; I just needed a little pick me up. Isn't that what coffee is all about? I was in a hurry so I promised to see him at the auto wrecker's and headed out the door.

I opened the garage door and of course, I took a few seconds to admire my car. It was going to need a wash. The road grime and dust was starting to accumulate. It also needed gas. That's why I was drinking coffee from a travel mug – to save time. I drove to the nearest service station and pulled in. Over the years, a number of my elders told me that buying a car was the cheapest part of ownership. Keeping it running took the real money. Like almost everyone else my age, I did not believe them. I was about to learn the truth. I had a choice between full and self-serve. I chose self-service, the cheaper of the two. I had forty-five dollars in my wallet, more than enough for a tank of gas and a couple of hamburgers later on, right. Twenty-five, thirty, thirty-five, the meter kept spinning with no end in sight. When it approached forty, I eased up the nozzle. At forty-two I stopped. My two hamburgers were now a bag of nacho chips and the gas gauge only showed three-quarters of a tank. Lesson learned; listen to your elders.

I was going to have to work a few more hours to keep gas in the car, but it was worth it. No gas-sipping sub-compact for me. Women, wimps and welfare recipients drove a Sun Fire, Focus, or Neon; hard working men did not. I know! I know that's not cool. I didn't really believe what I was saying, but somehow, I had to justify driving a gas-guzzler. I went inside to pay for the gas and would you believe it, they threw in a free car wash. Like I would risk the Monte Carlo's pristine finish in their outdated automatic carwash complete with paint scratching brushes.

I picked up Laura and Tracy, and thanks to my early departure, we arrived at school right on time. Hey wait a minute! There is something wrong here. Didn't owning a car mean that you needed less time to get from point A to point B? So then, why did I have to leave early? I guess maybe I learned another lesson today.

The morning passed quietly, but at noon Tracy ran to meet us in front of Laura's locker. She was waving a couple of sheets of paper. "Mel, you've got to read this. Dan Carruthers got a promotion."

As a part of her new duties, Tracy was required to check the local news on the internet. She was looking for stories involving the school and its students. This morning she came across the article about Dan and knowing that I would be interested she printed off a copy.

I wasn't surprised to learn Dan received a promotion, even if I did not think he deserved it. Joe told me the night of the fire that Dan was expecting a bump in pay. What surprised me was the position he was promoted to. Dan wasn't promoted to inspector. He wasn't promoted to assistant this or that. He was made head of the Crimes against Property department. The article quoted the mayor, the chief of police and for some reason, the head of security at the pharmaceutical company.

They all had nothing but praise for Dan. The mayor alluded to Dan's long and illustrious career as a community police officer. The police chief talked about Dan's outstanding arrest record that led to an above-average number of convictions. Most of the article was dedicated to the comments of Chris Raymond. Chris was introduced as the recently-hired head of security at Parkfield Pharmaceuticals. Chris admitted that he was new to the region and didn't know Dan Carruthers that well. "In the short time that I have known him, he has shown that he is an outstanding police officer and an even more outstanding citizen. He has dedicated himself to serving your community. Thanks to Dan's endeavours, a major theft of my company's products was averted. If those drugs had reached the street, hundreds and possibly thousands of people, might have been injured. Dan was tireless in this investigation even while attending classes in an attempt to make himself a better officer. His record shows that he spent dozens of hours of his own time running down leads. That's right ladies and gentlemen; he spent his own time running down leads. Right now, there is a man on the run, thanks to Dan. A murderer is running for his life and you can bet the citizens of Parkfield have nothing to fear from him, thanks to Dan. This man is a hero and deserves to be rewarded. With Dan as its head, the Crimes against Property department will be stronger, leaner and meaner. Within a very short time, I am sure that Dan's positive attitude and strong work ethic will have a rejuvenating effect on the other members in the department. It will make criminals think twice before they try anything in our city. With this in mind, I, and the management of Parkfield Pharmaceuticals, took an unprecedented step and approached the mayor and chief of police and encouraged them to name our friend and colleague, Dan Carruthers the head of Crimes against Property, a position recently left vacant because of a retirement. In addition to putting our support behind Dan, we have agreed to contribute a substantial amount of money towards crime prevention."

The Dan Carruthers, this Raymond guy was talking about, was not the Officer Carruthers I knew. He didn't appear to be all that hard a worker. Most of his time was spent sitting in his cruiser or the donut shop. Was making threats to girls considered working on his own time? What about the story Laura told me? Was that a fine and upstanding police officer? Joe Grosjean, a co-worker of Dan's, wasn't impressed with his abilities. My uncle and some of his friends, people who were familiar with the police for all the wrong reasons, had nothing good to say about him. So why was he being promoted? Was it any of my business?

The girls and I spent the rest of the noon hour discussing Dan and his promotion. I decided to make it my business to know more about Dan. He had threatened me. In his own way, he threatened the girls and if that wasn't enough, my father's life and reputation were at stake. According to Dan, my father had not only planned the theft of drugs, but was also a murderer on the run. The problem was: what do I do?

Laura, with more than a little help from Tracy, convinced me that the internet was the place to start. In this day and age, there were few secrets. I reminded them that my computer was at the police station. "No problem," said Tracy. "Do you still have internet access? If you do, I will borrow a lap top from my Dad's store and we can use that to check on Dan."

We had a plan. After work I would pick them up and we would go back to my place and start our search.

Thank heavens, it was busy at work. I worked overtime, almost an hour, and had twelve dollars in tips to show for it. I was late picking up the girls. I tried to explain but I was assured it wasn't an issue. Tracy had a laptop with her. Thanks to her father and his electronic store, it was the newest, most up-to-date version available. We left their parents my home phone number and promised to be good.

Before driving home, we checked out the two houses that were on our list from the night before. I noticed a blue truck pull into a parking spot about three houses away, but thought nothing of it. It was more than likely someone getting home from work. Laura tried knocking on the doors we were interested in, but no one was home at either of them. As soon as we arrived at the house, I turned on the television hoping to catch one of the local news casts. As luck would have it, we missed them by a few minutes. If we hadn't wasted our time checking on Tom's neighbours... Oh, well better luck next time.

The girls had already eaten supper so they went to work on the computer while I made a sandwich. I already missed my mother's home cooking. I opened up the bag of nachos I purchased that morning and poured them in a bowl before taking them to the living room where the girls had the lap top set up.

"We need a printer," was the first thing Tracy said.

I pointed to the printer on the desk where my computer once sat. Maybe Tracy was an expert on the computer, but from what I could see Laura was no slouch either. Tracy went to the printer, read off a series of numbers and before I knew it the printer was spewing out a stream of paper. The clattering lasted all of two and half minutes and then it quit. I was out of paper. I searched the house and found a few sheets. I loaded them up and noticed that the printer was out of ink. What next!

After Tracy made a call, Laura worked some more magic and punched in another series of numbers that Tracy gave her. When she was finished with the call Tracy turned to me and said, "We'll be able to pick up our copies at the store tomorrow. I chose the store instead of the house, because the ink is a lot cheaper on the big industrial printer. Don't worry; it won't cost you anything either way, but I promised my father I would save money where I could."

What could I say but Thank You! Thank You! Thank You! The information that Laura was digging up appeared endless. There was article after article on Dan Carruthers. Thanks to an informant this person was arrested. Thanks to an eye witness that Dan Carruthers located, that person was arrested. Laura even found an article describing the arrest of one George Crawford. The crime was painting graffiti on a park bench. The arresting officer was none other than our friend Officer Carruthers. According to the article, Dan Carruthers credited an un-named informant for the arrest.

As a result of that article, George Crawford was added to our list of people to talk to. Once Laura found everything there was to find about Dan Carruthers, she went to work on Tom Crawford. Time after time, she pressed the print icon and in my imagination I could hear the printer, clear across town, clicking and clacking away.

I heard a vehicle drive into the lane. Looking out the window, I saw that it was my uncle. As I watched him climb out of his car, I noticed a blue truck parked down near the corner. Was it the same truck? Probably, it was not.

Uncle Sid saw the computer and the papers spread out on the end table. He asked what we were up to and I told him. "The news starts in a few minutes and we are going to see if there is an update," I told him.

While we waited for the news, we talked about Dan. My uncle had a lot to say on the subject. Dan and his informants were well known on the street. According to my uncle, many of his informants were legitimate people willing to squeal on others for money, or to protect themselves. Uncle Sid knew of others who were not as legitimate, people who were blackmailed into informing for Dan. Dan would give his theory on the crime and then insist that his informant back him up. If you co-operated, you might get a small reward, but often enough you didn't even see that. If you didn't co-operate, you were harassed, and more than one unco-operative informant was arrested because of evidence planted by the police.

We asked for names to add to our list, although I was doubtful my uncle would give them to me. I was surprised when he agreed to talk to those involved and see if they would come forward.

The early news was just starting so we all sat quietly and waited for the broadcast to begin. Dan's promotion was the lead story. Dan stood near a makeshift podium while the mayor, police chief, and Chris Raymond took their turns speaking. The reporter, whose article we read, got the words right but the television camera told more. The police chief was an uncomfortable man. Only after some prodding from the mayor, did he step up to the podium. You would have thought he was eating limes, by the sour look on his face, a look that did not go away while he read from his prepared speech. Chris Raymond, on the other hand looked right at home, which indeed he was – the podium was sitting on the lawn in front of the Parkfield Pharmaceutical office, its huge logo prominently displayed.

I was caught off guard when Dan approached the microphone. The article I read didn't quote Dan at all. It was soon apparent why. Dan had nothing new to say. He repeated his earlier words almost verbatim. He had a few new nasty things to say about my father and added a couple of sentences describing how he was going to use his new position to bring crime in our city to its knees. By the time, he was finished even the mayor had a doubtful look about him. I turned the television off in anger.

It was Uncle Sid who brought up the subject of Parkfield Pharmaceutical. "What do they have to do with this? How much money are they donating anyway? It must be a lot if they convinced the mayor to fall for this tripe. Why Dan? What has he done for them? I cannot imagine why they are singling him out for praise. There must have been other officers involved.

Besides, I don't know why they are preaching against crime on television when they are hiring people to work in the plant that not even I would hire. You don't even have to apply. I know of three guys who were literally approached on the street and offered jobs. All of them have records as long as my arm. Theft, drugs, assault - you name it, they have done it.

Laura added a couple of new names to her list - Parkfield Pharmaceutical and Chris Raymond. They would have to wait for another day. It was getting late and it was time for me to drive Laura and Tracy home. It was, after all, a school night. I was not going to have them home one minute later than their parent's expected. The Torino's were good to me and I had no intention of making them angry.

I backed out of the yard and once I was on the street, I remembered to check for the blue truck. I glanced in my rear view mirror. A vehicle was sitting there, but I couldn't identify it because its headlights were on.

CHAPTER SIXTEEN

The trip to drop the girls off was uneventful. I kept an eye on my rear-view mirror. There was always a set of headlights behind me but after all, this was a city. Cities have traffic, even at night. If someone was following me, they kept their distance. The only vehicles that drove up close enough to be identified turned off soon after. When I was on my block once more, I noticed that the blue truck was gone.

The following morning I awoke to the smell of coffee. Uncle Sid was sitting at the kitchen table with his coffee cup and the morning paper in front of him. Before pouring my own coffee, I carried an armful of dirty clothes to the basement and threw them in the washer. If my timing was right, I would be able to throw the newly-washed clothes in the dryer before heading off to school.

Once the washer was humming along nicely, I returned to the kitchen and my coffee. I sat at the table and glanced suspiciously between my uncle and the paper and commented, "I didn't know we had the paper delivered."

Giving me a sheepish look, he said, "I found it lying near the front door. I guess one of the neighbourhood dogs must have dragged it over,"

I glanced out the window to see if there were any strange vehicles. There wasn't a strange vehicle or a dog in sight. I did see my neighbour, wearing nothing but a bath robe, in his front yard looking in his flower garden and under the bushes that separated our properties. I was quite sure he wasn't going to find what he was searching for. Thank heavens, Tracy wasn't around. I'm almost positive she would have been able to follow the tracks my uncle left when he stole the paper.

I summoned up a deep dark frown which I cast his way hoping to convey my displeasure. He got the message, because he gave me a slight nod before handing me the local news section of the paper. There was nothing new. The police were still looking for my father; Dan Carruthers was going to make changes at the police station, not all of them popular; and Parkfield Pharmaceutical was hiring.

Because I was driving to school, not walking, I had a few extra minutes of leisure. I thought of yesterday and my grumbling because I had to leave early to buy gas. I guess all things do work out in the end. I remembered the washing machine. By the time it finished and I transferred the clothes to the dryer, I was late leaving home.

I picked up the girls, Laura first of course, although it was a little quicker to pick Tracy up first. They directed me to a strip mall downtown. I was familiar with the mall. One of my favourite stores was located here. ST Electronics was the anchor tenant. I visited it often, buying a few odds and ends when I had the money, but mostly I just wandered the aisles wishing I could afford to purchase just a few of its many treasures. Large screen TVs, surround-sound, computers, cameras, stereos, fridges, stoves – they had it all.

To my surprise, Tracy told me to stop when we neared it. I parked and she ran inside returning a minute later with a handful of papers. Then it dawned on me. This was the electronics store that was owned by Tracy's father. I stammered out my thoughts to Laura.

"I'm sorry," she said. "I thought I told you. ST stands for Steve Torino, Tracy's father. They have owned this place for years, since it opened as a matter of fact."

By the time Laura was finished with her explanation, Tracy was back in the car. If I did not hurry, we were going to be late for class. I had a choice to speed or be late. I chose the second option. Someday, I would risk a speeding ticket. How else would I find out what the Monte Carlo was made out of? In my books, however, being on time for class did not warrant a fine.

The bell was ringing when we pulled up to the school and we could see a steady stream of students heading for the classrooms. I made one circuit around the parking lot and wouldn't you know it, it was full. I stopped near the front doors and let the girls out. I spent the next ten minutes trying to find a parking space. The closest one was nearly three blocks away. Wow, owning a vehicle did have its challenges!

We spent the lunch hour going over the papers we printed off. We didn't learn a whole lot. Dan Carruthers was a cop and Tom Crawford was a crook. Dan had made a few arrests here and there. Tom was charged with committing a few crimes here and there. We found nothing that connected them except the George Crawford incident.

There was nothing at all about George, aside from the graffiti and his refusal to pay Tom's funeral expenses. We had no idea where he lived, where he worked, or even, if he was still in town. All in all, we were no closer to saving my father's reputation. We were not going to be any closer at the end of the day either. Tracy had work to do at the school and Laura was going to help her. I had my job at the auto wrecker's and a couple of other chores to do. Our sleuthing would have to wait a day or so. It wasn't as though someone's life was at stake. The city's secrets would be safe for one more day.

I arrived at work to find a semi-truck load of wrecked cars waiting for my attention. A lot of the wrecks in the yard were bought at auction sales. If someone wrecked their car to such an extent that it was cheaper to sell it for its parts than to fix it, the insurance company paid the replacement cost of the vehicle and then took possession of the wreck. The insurance companies then resold these wrecks as salvage for whatever price someone was willing to pay. The buyers were usually auto wreckers like the one I worked for. The load of vehicles in the yard told me that my uncle or his partner must have attended one of these sales recently. I suspected that it wasn't Uncle Sid, or he would have mentioned it. It did not matter who bought the cars, it was now my job to take an inventory of the parts that might be available for resale and then find a place to keep the wreck where it was accessible to remove the parts. There were four cars, two trucks and two SUV's in today's load. At one time, it would have taken me a week to sort everything out. Now, well, let's see, I estimated I would be finished by quitting time.

One of the cars was a Firebird. It was the same model as Scott's, but it was a couple of years newer. One of the front fenders was destroyed, as was the headlight, grill and hood. It was expensive to fix if you were an insurance company, but was relatively cheap if you had a ready supply of parts. The rest of the car was in pretty good shape. It even started and ran when I hooked it up to a battery. It gave me an idea.

I went to work on the trucks and SUV's. One of the SUV's wasn't too bad. I hoped they didn't pay much for the others because there wasn't much left of them. Fifteen minutes before quitting time, I took my list inside. My uncle wasn't around, but his partner was. He took the list from me and spent several minutes going over it. When he was finished, he told me to grab a seat.

I was afraid I made a mistake, but he put my fears to rest when he said, "I'm impressed at how accurate your list is. I spent some time prior to the sale going over those vehicles and I did not find much more than you did. As you know, the value of the vehicle depends on the value of its parts. At the auction, you only have a few minutes to decide how much to bid and you are bidding against some very knowledgeable people. Finding a salvageable part that everyone else misses can mean money in our pocket and thinking a part is salvageable when it isn't can cost us money. You are learning this business as fast as anyone I know. Someday, I hope to take you to a sale with me."

His praise meant a lot to me. It also made what I had to say easier. "What's the story on the Firebird you bought?"

"The boys at Central Motors want to build a stock car for racing," he told me. "They asked me to find them a car. I've been looking for something like the Firebird for quite a while. It was a little more money than they wanted to spend, but it is all I have been able to find."

The Central Motors gang wanted a chassis. They didn't care about the fenders, the interior or the motor. They would be replacing all of those. What they needed was Scott's beat up piece of junk. I made a deal with my boss. He would have his guys in the shop fix up this Firebird using parts from Scott's. I would give him, on Scott's behalf, the thousand dollars he paid for his Firebird at auction. In return for the work his guys did on the car, he could sell Scott's Firebird to Central Motors. He took only a moment to think about it before he agreed.

Instead of going home to wash the Monte Carlo, I found myself at the mall. I hoped Scott hadn't locked up his kiosk and gone home. I took a cursory look around the parking lot while finding a place to park and didn't see the Firebird. Not a good sign. I did see a blue truck pulling into a parking spot not far from the one I chose. I was starting to worry about that truck.

Scott was still at his kiosk dealing with a couple of customers. I waved to let him know I was around and then I went to an ATM and took out fifty dollars to replace the money I spent on gas the day before. Scott was still busy, so I went to the food court and ordered a submarine sandwich to go. By the time my sandwich was ready, Scott was getting ready to close up.

"Hey Malcolm," he said with his infectious grin. "I don't suppose I can get a ride home. The Firebird is dead again. I was about to call home for a ride, but if you are going my way it will save them the trip."

"No problem," I said. "I'm here to talk to you about the Firebird. We can chat on the way."

Once we were on the road, I told him about the Firebird at work. I even drove past the wrecking yard so he could have a look at it. The paint on the replacement fenders weren't going to match, but I told him that the people who helped me paint the Monte Carlo would probably help him as well.

One peek at the newer Firebird was all it took to convince him to write out a check. "The sooner they get the old Firebird out of the yard, the better. My mother is really getting on my case about it. She says that it is an eyesore. I will pay the tow charges, if they can pick it up," he said.

Scott's mother was tending to some flowers in her front yard when we pulled up. She gave Scott a hug and to my chagrin after Scott made introductions she had a hug for me as well. "Stay for supper," she insisted. "The barbecues on and there's lots of food."

I could smell the barbecue and believe me it smelled nice. My submarine sandwich would keep until tomorrow, so I agreed to stay. I noticed a phone hanging on the garage wall. Scott noticed me looking and told me to go ahead and use it. I called one of the tow truck drivers from work. He assured me that Scott's Firebird would be picked up tomorrow morning, at the latest. As a favour to me, there would be no charge. Scott overheard the conversation as did his mother.

Scott told her about the deal he made. "Any deal is a good deal if it means that piece of junk is no longer in my yard," she replied.

Scott's father was tending the barbecue on the back yard deck. We walked around back to say hello and he pointed to a couple of lawn chairs. "Take a load off. Supper will be ready soon," he said.

I asked Scott how work was going. He assured me all was well. It was doing so well that in a couple of months he was going to start looking for an apartment of his own. Mr. Morgan piped in, "Before you move anywhere, you are going to find someone you can trust to help you out at the newsstand. You are working seven days a week and that has to stop. Maybe Malcolm here knows someone who is willing to work weekends. Would one of the girls, who were with you the other day, be looking for a job?"

I knew that neither Laura nor Tracy was looking for a job. Laura worked at the movie theatre and Tracy was busy with her activities at school. I did know someone who was job hunting though. Brandon, the boy who approached me at the school to thank me for my help with the bullies, wanted a job. Brandon was not picked on because he was weak. He was not picked on because he was a sissy. He was picked on, because he was taught from an early age, to turn the other cheek. That, and the fact his clothes were old and out of fashion, made him an easy target for the school toughs.

I told the Morgan's what I knew about Brandon. "Send him around. He sounds just like the person I have been looking for," said Scott. "What about you? Hear any word from your father?"

I was telling him about our internet searches that were, for the most part, fruitless, when a car pulled into a driveway a few doors down. Scott returned its occupant's wave. "Maybe he can help you. He's a reporter at the local paper."

I was willing to try anything, so I walked with Scott over to the neighbour's. Scott told the reporter who I was and what I was up to.

"Funny meeting you here," he said when Scott finished. "The strangest thing just happened at the paper. A couple of us were going to do an in-depth story on the drug company and the recent events. We went to the editor with our proposal and were told to leave it alone. He went so far as to send me on an out-of-town assignment. I'm leaving just as soon as I can pack. I'm in a hurry, but we can talk when I get back in a few days. In the meantime, you might want to call the Motor Vehicle Branch and the Land Titles Office. A lot of their information is there for the asking."

I thanked him for his time and after saying so long to Scott, I drove home.

CHAPTER SEVENTEEN

Wednesday and Thursday passed slowly. Outside of school, I found little opportunity to spend time with Laura. School assignments, my job at the auto wrecker's, grocery shopping and life, in general, kept me busy.

The assignment that was on one of the flash drives confiscated by the police was due on Thursday, so I made a point of contacting the lawyer to see if I was going to get it back. An hour later, the lawyer returned my call. He told me that the police refused to give me the flash drive. He gave me some legal mumbo jumbo - they could keep it for up to two weeks or was it two months or maybe even two years, I don't remember. The upshot of it was; he could not get it back. He suggested I talk nice to a friendly police officer and maybe he would print me a copy of my assignment. Did this lawyer hear a thing that I said on my first visit? I would not have needed his help in the first place if it were not for unfriendly police. It was now too late to rewrite the paper, even if I wanted to. Had I wanted to rewrite it, I would have started the process several days earlier. Instead, I took the easy route by procrastinating, hoping that the lawyer would take care of the problem for me. Look where that got me.

I was left with no choice, but to call Joe Grosjean. I used a pay phone so that I wouldn't be identified by call display if one of Dan Carruthers cronies answered. A gruff voice picked up the phone on the eighteenth ring. Yes, it was eighteen; I counted, because I didn't have anything better to do standing in that phone booth. "What do you want?" the voice asked.

I asked for Joe Grosjean. "Try the Parks Department," and we were cut off.

I no longer had to worry about being identified, so I opted to make the call from home. It was now well past eight p.m. and I really did not expect anyone to answer the phone so imagine my surprise when Joe picked up. I told him who I was and asked why he was at the Parks department office.

"Dan has not forgiven me for sticking up for you the night of the fire, and to punish me he has assigned me to park duty. I spend my nights patrolling the city's parks making sure no one is defacing them, camping in them or using them to make out. It isn't as bad as some of my predecessors make it out to be, but it can get boring. What can I help you with?" he asked.

I told him why I called. He told me that he could not make any promises, but he would see what he could do. I told him which flash drive I was interested in, and gave him the information that he needed to locate the assignment.

Twenty minutes later, he called me back. One of the guys on duty has agreed to print off your assignment. He does not want anyone to know he is helping you or me, for that matter, so you will have to meet him away from the police station. He is making a donut run at nine-thirty if you want to meet him at the donut shop. I happily agreed to the arrangements and even more happily, thanked Joe for his trouble.

I was late making the rendezvous. I left home with lots of time to spare, but the moment I backed out onto the street, I was surrounded by police cars. They spent the next half-hour going through my car from one end to the other. I asked the officer, who appeared to be in charge, what was happening. We had an anonymous tip that you are transporting drugs. Either you tell us where you have them hid, or we will tear this car apart. Of course, I couldn't tell him where the non-existent drugs were so I watched in horror as they began throwing things out of my prized Monte Carlo.

I guess it might have been worse. They didn't tear out the seats, rip out the dash or destroy the door panels. They checked every nook and cranny though. They opened up the CD cases and threw them on the sidewalk when they found no contraband. They took out the floor mats, but thank goodness, they didn't cut the carpets. They checked the trunk. The lawn was littered with my spare tire, tools and other odds and ends that I kept, in case the car broke down. In the end, they found nothing. There was no apology and Dan's old partner even had the nerve to laugh and say, "See you tomorrow."

I didn't have time to replace everything, so I left it piled in the yard while I drove to the donut shop. To my relief there was a squad car idling in the parking lot. I drove up beside it and the driver rolled down his window. It was an officer I did not recognize. "Are you Malcolm," he asked?

I told him I was. I started to apologize for being late but he cut me off. "I heard on the radio that they were giving some punk kid the old drug search run-around. After my conversation with Joe, I thought it might be you so I decided to give you a few extra minutes. I hope they didn't break anything."

I found myself in a bit of a predicament. It was starting to rain, so I was in a hurry to leave, but I didn't want to appear rude. This nice guy does me a huge favour and I have to brush him off. What could I say? I told him I didn't think anything was ruined, but I had not taken the time to check. I told him about the pile of belongings that was waiting for me in the yard.

Instead of being offended by my abruptness, he told me that I had better get on my way. I left, but not before I asked him his name. "Alan Wilkins. My friends call me Al," he replied.

The stereo, all of a sudden, conked out on me when I was about half way home. I needed music, so I was going to have to try and fix it but first things first. My things were still piled up in the yard, so I carried them to the garage. Once they were safely out of the rain, I turned to the stereo. It was a simple fix. One of the cops must have been pulling on the face plate and loosened a connection. I reconnected the wires and voilà I had music. I was going to sleep better knowing that my stereo was fixed. Once the rain stopped, it only took me a few minutes to put everything back in the car where it belonged. The rain washed some of the dust off the Monte Carlo, but it didn't wash off the bugs or road grime. Tomorrow I was going to wash it, no matter what.

Tomorrow came sooner than I planned. Despite my relief that I had music, sleep was illusive. What was happening with my father? Did he need help? Was he expecting me or someone else in the family to come to his aid? Should I be trying harder to find him? He disappeared two weeks ago. Was it only two weeks? I missed him and wanted to see him, no matter what he may have done.

At five a.m. I gave up and got out of bed. The sun had barely appeared when I went outside to wash the car. The first thing I noticed was the cop car parked at the corner. Dollars to donuts, it was there to keep an eye on me. I spent the next hour and a half washing, vacuuming and then waxing the car. If I may say so, it looked good when I was finished. I said good morning to the neighbour when he came outside to pick up his morning paper. He ignored me.

By eight o'clock, the lack of sleep was starting to catch up with me. I drank my third cup of coffee while I got ready for school. I was going to need the caffeine to get me through the day.

School was quiet. I handed in my assignment. I was one of only two students to have the paper finished, so the teacher extended the due date by a week. All that worrying, sweating and running around last night was for nothing. Life is not fair!

There were no classes scheduled for the next day. The teachers had a conference, or something to attend. I really did not care where they went as long as I got the day off. The fact that it was a Friday was a bonus.

After I finished work at the wrecker's, I cleaned up as best I could and drove to Laura's. We were going to help out at the theatre tonight, and in return, Laura would be free to do as she liked on Saturday night. The theatre was busy for a week night. According to Laura, it was normal to be busy on the night before a school holiday. This week's movie was an animated family flick. There were dozens of cute little animals running around trying to stay out of the clutches of an evil hunter. In the end, the hunter was caught in one of his own traps and all the animals lived happily ever after. All in all, it wasn't a bad movie. Did I mention that we were sitting at the very back of the balcony and I kissed Laura for the first time?

By the time I got home, I was so tired that despite my very fond memories of that kiss, I managed to sleep through an earthquake, literally. My father's name was nowhere to be found in the morning news. That day's big news was the earthquake. According to those in the know, it maxed out at 4.6 on the Richter scale. Not strong as earthquakes go, but in an area like ours that never had an earthquake before it was definitely news worthy.

I met Laura and Tracy at the coffee shop. One look at Laura and I was reminded of last night's kiss. Another look and I wanted to kiss her again. I looked around and decided this was not the time or place. I took her hand instead. The girls enjoyed hot chocolate and I enjoyed a coffee - double/double if you please - while we decided how we were going to spend our day.

I told them about the reporter's suggestion that we go to the Motor Vehicle and Land Title offices. Just as she did a few evenings back, Laura took a few minutes to apply a little make-up and put on the jacket that made her look a good five to ten years older. I drove to the Motor Vehicle office that was the closest and Laura took our list of names and went inside.

Tracy entertained me with stories of growing up in the Torino family while we waited. I was so engrossed in what she was saying that I didn't realize that a half hour had passed since Laura left. Just as I was getting out of the car to search for her, she came walking up.

Tracy asked her how she made out. "Dan owns two vehicles and his wife owns one. He has a blue Dodge truck - that'll be the one he was driving at your place that day. He just bought a new SUV a week ago and his wife owns a car. Tom didn't own a vehicle. He wrecked his last one about six months ago and never registered a replacement. George owns an older sedan and someone who lives at the same address, his wife or daughter owns a minivan. Chris Raymond owns a truck, SUV and a camper. I have their home addresses as well, if you want to check them out.

We went for a drive around the city, all the way around the city. The addresses we had were scattered from one end of town to the other. Dan lived in a middle class area of town. We had trouble finding his house. It looked exactly the same as every other house on the street. They all had small yards, no garages and very few of them had fences. When we finally found Dan's house, none of his vehicles were parked near it. We even checked the back alley. At that time of day you would expect two of the vehicles to be gone. Dan and his wife had to get to work somehow, but where was the third vehicle. We knew that there was no one else living there with a driver's licence because Laura checked. We drove around the block one more time in case we missed it, but there was nothing.

Chris Raymond must have been making good money because he had a nice house. The Torino's all lived in nice houses in a nice part of town, but Chris' house was even nicer. We noticed the truck right away. It was backed up to the camper. It may have even been hooked to the camper. The SUV was gone.

Our next destination was George Crawford's residence. The Raymond camper was worth more than George's home. George lived in a trailer park on the outskirts of town. If a person was generous, he might say that this trailer park was run-down. If he was realistic, he would call it a dump. George's mobile home was no better or worse than any of his neighbour's. I still would not want to have to live there. I could not help but notice the looks of horror on Laura and Tracy's faces.

Tracy said it best, "People live in places like this." It was obvious they did. Kids were playing in the street and many of the homes had lights showing in the windows. The minivan that was registered to the Crawford's, was sitting up on blocks. Its engine could be seen sitting in the cargo area. The sedan was nowhere around.

It was close to lunch time, so we drove to a fast food restaurant. Tracy was still haunted by what she saw in the trailer park. "I've always taken the ability to afford restaurants, vacations and what-not for granted. I won't do that again. I might just have to say a prayer of thanks before I eat my burger." That is all that was said, but I could not help but notice the few moments of silence before we dug into our meal.

After lunch, we tried out the Land Title office. Once again, it took about a half an hour for Laura to return. To no one's surprise, we learned that George didn't own any other property. He didn't even own the property that his mobile home sat on. He rented it.

The only property that Tom owned was the now-burned house. Dan owned a cottage near the lake where we went swimming the previous weekend, and Chris Raymond owned a cottage and another rural property. According to Laura, there were no houses, just outbuildings, on this property. I asked if she knew how to find it. With a flourish she pulled a map out of her pocket. "It is all right here," she said.

Checking it out would have to wait for another day. By the time I dropped the girls off, it would be time for me to go to work.

As usual, I dropped Tracy off first. I parked in Laura's driveway and was reaching out to enfold her in my arms so that I could get a repeat of last night's kiss when her father walked around the corner of the house pushing a lawnmower. It was not the right time or place again. This was killing me.

CHAPTER EIGHTEEN

I woke up bright and early on Saturday morning. I was expected at the auto wrecker's and to be quite honest, even if I was not expected; I would have shown up hoping to pick up a couple of hours work at least. Money was a bit of an issue. More than a week, almost two had passed since I found the money on the kitchen counter. My mom had yet to send me any, but when I talked to her on the phone the previous evening, she promised she would. Uncle Sid's only contribution so far was a fridge full of a beer.

Even though Uncle Sid was nowhere to be seen, I made a pot of coffee. I'll admit I am officially hooked on the stuff. I even went so far as to fill one of my father's thermoses to take to work with me.

The wrecking yard was busy even for a Saturday. It was three o'clock before I had time to check on the progress of Scott's Firebird. I was impressed with the guys in the shop. They were almost finished putting it back together. They promised me that they would finish no later than Sunday morning, but they hoped to finish that night. I called Scott with the news.

"That is great," he said. "I'll come by with pizzas for them just as soon as I lock up. How many are working?"

I told him there were three of them working on the car and then I got to the real reason I called him. "How did the interview with Brandon go? The last time I talked to Brandon he told me that he was going to meet with you on Wednesday. Since then I have not spoken to either of you."

"Fantastic! He's here with me now. He's been training the past two days and tomorrow afternoon I am going to leave him here alone. Thanks for sending him my way. I owe you big time, both for Brandon, and for the Firebird."

We chatted until I noticed the boss leave his office. I was not all that worried about him catching me on the phone, but I was interested in the pay cheques that he was handing out. As befitted the youngest employee, I received mine last. It was worth the wait. After our conversation earlier in the week, he must have decided to give me a raise. It wasn't a huge raise but every little bit helps, right!

After a stop at home to clean up and change my clothes, I picked Laura up at her parents. It was to be our first official date, just the two of us. To be polite, I invited Tracy to join us, but with a wink and a nudge she told me that her hair needed washing. It could wait no longer. It had to be washed that night.

Laura and I went to a nice restaurant for a bite to eat. It wasn't a four-star restaurant – I couldn't afford one of those – but it was not Burger King either. We enjoyed the meal, and at Laura's suggestion, we even shared a dessert, chocolate cheese cake. We lingered at the table as long as we could. We were lost in one another's company. When the waiter brought the bill and suggested that I could pay him now, I realized it was time to leave.

What do two sixteen-year-olds do on a Saturday night? The movies were out of the question. Laura worked at a theatre and had no desire to spend her night off at one. We were not old enough to go to bars. Where can you go dancing except at bars? Neither of us was a fan of roller-blading. There was a high school basketball game on, but we were not prepared to face that issue just yet. We decided to go bowling. We were not very good at it, but we had a good time just the same. We laughed, joked and talked. For a couple of hours, I did not have a care in the world. No police to worry about. My father was not a criminal. I was just a normal teenager spending time with a pretty girl.

All good things must come to an end, and that evening was no exception. Laura was supposed to be home by midnight. We planned on stopping for ice cream, so at eleven-fifteen we went out to the Monte Carlo. I opened the passenger door for Laura. Aren't I just the real gentleman though? I got the idea from a movie that I had watched when I was a kid. I got in the driver's side and started the car. I put my foot on the brake and was about to put the Monte Carlo in gear when something stopped me. The brakes did not feel right. I pumped them a couple of times with the car still in park. They were spongy and on the third pump, the pedal went right to the floor.

I fished a flashlight out of the pile of stuff I unceremoniously threw into the trunk a couple of nights before. On the ground, at the front passenger side, was a puddle. There was another puddle on the other side. I didn't want to ruin my pants, so I carefully got down on my knees and dipped the tip of my finger into the liquid. One sniff and I knew what it was, brake fluid!

How could that be? The brake lines were brand new. Why would both of them fail at the same time? By the time I figured out what the problem was, not only were my pants ruined, but my shirt was ruined as well. I had to lie down on the pavement, and with the aid of the flashlight, I noticed that someone had used a pair of side cutters or something similar to sever both brake lines.

I spent a couple more minutes rummaging in the trunk and managed to locate what I was looking for, a piece of rubber hose and some hose clamps. It wasn't a long term fix, but it would last until I found more brake lines. Once the lines were back together, I refilled the brake fluid reservoir with fluid purchased at a nearby gas station. I had Laura pump the brakes a few times, while I bled the air from the lines. All in all, it took me forty-five minutes to make the repair and another five minutes to drive Laura home.

When Laura's parents learned what happened, they forgave her for being a few minutes late getting home. They insisted that I phone the police and make a report. I made the call and I guess the report was filled out. The officer, who took my call, didn't sound all that enthused about taking my information. He sounded even less enthused when I told him my name.

Our first official date ended with a peck on the cheek from Laura. It was not the way I wanted the evening to end, but the words that Laura whispered in my ear, gave me much to look forward to.

On Sunday morning, I had toast and coffee at the kitchen table with my uncle. He was not feeling that great and when I opened the fridge to get the coffee creamer, I knew why. The fridge was no longer full of beer. My sympathy for him evaporated and I good-naturedly told him just that.

We talked a little about my father. I told him what I was up to as for as trying to locate him and he told me what he was doing. I did not realize how much time he was spending searching for my father until he named all of the people he contacted, either in person or by phone. So far neither of us was any further ahead in our search. I told Uncle Sid to be careful and reminded him of the threatening phone calls I received. He gave me a funny look so I tried to explain; I would feel guilty if something happened to you while you were trying to help me. I would not want to lose a father and you too.

The smile he gave me belied his stern words, "Look kid, I am a Webb. Your father is a Webb and you are a Webb. I am doing this for myself and the other Webb's as much as I am doing it for you." "Besides," he concluded, "I won't be all that easy to hurt." He left the room but not before letting loose a loud and toxic belch. "A little something to remember me by," he said.

A few minutes later, the phone rang. It was Laura. "Tracy wants to go to the bowling alley and look for clues. Can you pick us up?"

I wasn't going to argue with spending time with the girls, so I assured her I was on my way. The night before, I hadn't given any thought to looking for foot prints or what have you. I was more worried about fixing the car and getting Laura home on time. I would not have been able to see them in the dark anyway. Wait now! Maybe I am just trying to justify the fact that I forgot. It was more than likely too late to find anything now. If anything was there, I probably destroyed it while I was lying on my back, shuffling around. Nevertheless, we were going to give it a go.

I picked up the girls and drove to the parking lot. Tracy did not receive any help unloading her equipment. Laura and I were busy kissing. Tracy, bless her heart, did not seem to mind. It was, by far, the best kiss yet. It would have lasted a whole lot longer, if I could have thought of a way to kiss and breathe at the same time. I told you that I was new to this game.

Tracy headed straight for the spot where the car was parked the night before. It was easy to find because of the stain left by the brake fluid. Tracy found dozens of foot prints in the dust of the parking lot. None of them were deep enough to make impressions but that didn't stop her from snapping pictures. She started near the brake fluid stains and carefully worked back in all directions. She was a good sixty feet from her starting point when she shouted. I walked over, and lo and behold, there in all its glory, was the print of a shoe with a crack across its sole. Twenty feet further back, she found another. Now that she knew in what direction to look, she found several more. She followed them across the parking lot snapping away with her camera. In the far corner of the lot, almost as far away from my parking spot of the night before as you could get, she found the now familiar tire track.

There's no doubt that somebody wanted to hurt us, well, me anyway, and there was also no doubt that nobody in authority cared.

Our original plan was to spend the day checking out the properties we learned about on Friday. The rural properties were quite a distance away and I wasn't sure if I trusted my repairs to the brake lines. I decided to stay closer to town.

Dan Carruthers lived not too far away so we took a drive by his house. The new SUV and car were both parked in the driveway. The blue truck wasn't there. Tracy insisted on getting out and walking past the Carruthers' home. We picked her up at the other end of the block. "I saw them. I saw them both. That jerk, Dan, was watching TV. I saw him through the window. His wife went out the side door. She's puttering in the back yard. Someone else must be using the truck," she concluded.

Maybe someone else was using the truck or maybe it was in a repair shop. Who knew?

Laura suggested that we drive by the Raymond residence. "What's the point," I said. "We don't have anything on him except my uncle's belief that they are hiring people with records. What does that have to do with my father, Dan or even Tom Crawford?"

Instead I drove to Laura's. We spent the afternoon playing video games. It was Laura and I against Tracy and Laura's brother Bob. We kicked butt. We were about to start another game when Mrs. Torino yelled out that supper would be ready in ten minutes. We decided to wait until later to start our game. Tracy went to talk to her aunt and Bob went to wash up for supper. Laura and I were left at the computer. She logged on to one of those social network pages. You know the ones, I mean. They list your family, friends and acquaintances. There was nothing new on Laura's page but before she logged off I noticed something. Laura Torino was in a relationship, with none other than me, Malcolm Webb. I was as proud as a peacock, sorry, peafowl to learn this news and promptly updated my own status.

Before Laura left the network page, I asked her to check and see if the Parkfield Police had a page. Sure enough they did. Public relations and all that, I guess. Laura punched in Dan Carruthers' name and his profile popped up. Name, D.O.B., marital status, address, occupation, and wait, was that his place of birth. Dan wasn't born in Parkfield. He was born in Harmony, a community, an hour's drive away.

"Just for curiosity's sake, see if Parkfield Pharmaceutical has a page," I asked Laura. She typed in Parkfield Pharmaceutical. They also had a page. Their page listed their employees, maybe not all of them, but most of them at least. We scrolled through the list. We recognized a number of the names. Some of our fellow students had parents working at the plant. A couple of my distant relatives worked there, and one of Laura's uncle's on her mother's side was a production foreman. We noticed all of their names. Laura typed in the name, Chris Raymond.

Before his profile finished loading we were called to supper; spaghetti and meatballs-Italian style. There was salad; garlic toast; the whole works. The family even used bibs. That was entirely new to me. Some slurping was allowed. How can you enjoy spaghetti without slurping? I was encouraged to eat seconds which I readily agreed to; so much for bashfulness and watching one's waistline.

By the time we finished coffee, dessert and our general chit chat it was almost time for me to leave. There was school tomorrow, and if I planned on wearing clean clothes, I was going to have to do laundry. With those thoughts in the back of my mind, and thoughts of a few moments alone with Laura and the possibility of another kiss at the front of my mind, it is no wonder I forgot all about the social network page, Parkfield Pharmaceutical and Chris Raymond.

I didn't get the kiss that I so desperately wanted from Laura, but I got three pecks on the cheek - one from Laura, another from Tracy and one from Laura's mother. Oh well! There is always tomorrow. If I sound like a stuck record again; welcome to my life.

A police cruiser followed me all of the way home and parked on the street when I pulled into the garage. I could see its driver watching me as I walked inside. Where was he yesterday when my car was being vandalized?

I managed to get a load of clothes in the washing machine, but I fell asleep before it was ready to go in the dryer. It's a good thing I was a driver. Once again, I was going to need the few extra minutes that driving to school saved me.

CHAPTER NINETEEN

Monday morning arrived all too soon. I made it to school on time; in fact I walked in the door twenty-five seconds before the bell sounded. My clothes weren't quite dry, but they were dry enough to wear.

It was a normal school day, the new normal anyway. By new, I mean that instead of being taunted by the general population, I was ignored. By new, I mean that I no longer ate alone at lunch time. Laura always ate with me. Tracy often joined us, and on occasion Brandon, appeared as well. Lunch time that day was spent doing homework.

When I finished my regular work at the wrecking yard, I convinced my uncle to hang around so that I could work on the Monte Carlo. The shop was empty; Scott's car was finished and on the road. I could have completed the work at home, but the hoist in the shop made everything a whole lot easier to get at. I was finishing with the second brake line when the phone rang. I let it ring a number of times expecting Uncle Sid to pick it up. It kept ringing, so eventually I picked it up myself. I half-expected it to be a wrong number. Our business hours were well known and it was now more than two hours past closing time. I was surprised to hear Laura's voice.

"Malcolm, is that you," she asked?
"It's me; the one and only; God's gift to mankind," I joked.
I know I wasn't funny; Laura knew I wasn't funny; but she laughed anyway, just because she is a nice person. "Remember, when we were on the computer last night. Remember, we were checking names at Parkfield Pharmaceutical. Well, I went to use the computer a few minutes ago and it was still logged onto that page. Remember, we asked for Chris Raymond's profile. Did you know that Chris was born in Harmony, the same town as Dan Carruthers? I thought you might find that interesting. I wanted to catch you before you left work, in case you wanted to swing by here and do some more computer research."

I promised I would be there in a few minutes. I was locking up the gate to the compound when a car pulled up. It was Scott and his two-toned Firebird. The thing looked weird, but according to Scott it ran like a clock.

"I've been looking for you," he added. "I have a little something to say thank you for your help with the car." He handed me a hundred-dollar gift certificate to one of the two four-star restaurants in town. "Take a friend out for dinner. It's the least I can do."

I tried to give the certificate back to him, but he made it abundantly clear that he found my attempt offensive. I grudgingly accepted it. What else could I do?

I told Scott that Laura was expecting me and why. He asked if it was all right if he tagged along. Laura's parents weren't home, but I was sure they would not mind if Scott visited with me. Scott's name arose in more than one of our conversations, and I knew that they had nothing but the utmost respect for him and his beliefs.

It was Tracy who let us into the Torino house, greeting us both with her customary peck on the cheek and said that Laura was in the computer room. Scott managed the stairs without much difficulty, but every time I saw him and his crutches, I could not help but feel a little sympathy for him and a lot of hate for IEDs.

Laura was making notes as we entered the room. She noticed Scott and before I said anything she reassured me that he was more than welcome. "I've been doing some checking," she said. "Dan is a couple of years older than Chris. We know that from their profile pages. They don't list one another as friends, but that should not be surprising. After all, these are professional profiles not personal ones. I haven't noticed any names they have in common what-so-ever. I thought of checking school records, but there is nothing on the internet about Harmony High School."

"Try Nolan High School," said Scott. "I played basketball a few years ago and we played against the Harmony team quite often. They called themselves the Nolan Wolves. The school is named after one of their well-known citizens. Notice I said well-known, not famous or beloved. Legend has it that a man named Nolan fought off a pack of grey wolves with nothing but a stick. The story was started by a former mayor named - you guessed it, Nolan. He conveniently forgot that wolves are not native to this part of the country. There has never been another documented sighting of a wolf anywhere in the region. The Wyatt family insists that the story is balderdash. They say that Nolan was drunk and killed his own dog. Believe whichever story you want, but be aware that at the turn of the century, the school was called Wyatt High School."

It was a good story and we all laughed when he finished telling it. Laura wasted no time starting a search on Nolan High School. Within seconds, she was showing us page after page of yearbook photos. We used Dan's birth date to figure out when he might have attended high school. We were a year out, but we found his freshman class picture. Dan must have flunked a grade somewhere along the line. It wouldn't surprise me if he had, or am I just being mean.

We found Chris Raymond's picture exactly where we expected to find it. While looking at the other pictures on the page, I thought I recognized someone. The face was familiar but something wasn't quite right about it, until I looked at the name below it. It was George Crawford. He looked enough like his brother to catch my attention, but there were definite differences in their appearances. I pointed the name out to the others and immediately started searching for a picture of Tom. We found it. Tom graduated two years after his brother.

So, now we knew that the Crawford's, Dan Carruthers and Chris Raymond all grew up in Harmony. We didn't know if that meant anything. Were they somehow connected? George must know Chris. They went to school together. According to the yearbooks, all four of them attended the school at the same time for one year at least. We kept up our search. We wanted to connect them, somehow. We checked sports teams, debating clubs, the chess league, the bands-swing and jazz, the drama club and cadets. There was nothing.

It was Scott who suggested we pay George Crawford a visit. It made a certain amount of sense. There was no way Dan was going to talk to us. Tom was dead and Chris Raymond, well, for some reason I couldn't see him wanting to talk to us, even if we had a decorated war veteran along for the ride. The question was; should we even be talking to George? Was it safe? What would Laura and Tracy's parents think? I knew the answer to that. They would say we were getting in way over our heads, and we had no business chasing off on these tangents. The girls refused to listen to my concerns and refused to be left behind.

Tracy piped in, "You need us. I will bring some recording things and Laura can take notes. Pretend she is a reporter or something."

I looked to Scott. He raised his eye brows and shrugged. "It's eight-thirty. It's getting late. We might not get home before your parents." It was my last, and I hoped, best shot at convincing them to stay behind.

Laura grabbed her coat and said, "The longer we stand here arguing, the more likely that will happen. Let's get on with it."

Next thing I knew, we were all in the Monte Carlo and I was driving across town. The trailer court, that didn't look very nice in the daylight, looked even worse at night. I thought of the story Scott told earlier. Maybe wolves weren't native to this part of the country, but if anything was going to attract them, it would be the filth and vermin in neighbourhoods like this.

We had trouble finding George's mobile home. There was not one light working on his entire street. The only reason I found it, was because I recognized the minivan up on blocks. I stopped on the street. There was no place to park in the yard. I was about to climb out when the door of the trailer opened. I knew from the school picture that the man about to leave the trailer was George Crawford. He was a whole lot older now, and nowhere near as healthy-looking, but it was definitely him. I met him in his driveway. I was pretending that I was much older and more important than I actually was, when I asked if we could sit down and have an unofficial chat about his high school days.

I don't know if it was the poor lighting, or my good acting but he didn't see through me and agreed to talk. "It'll have to be at the coffee shop," he told me. "The wife gets off work in a few minutes and I have to pick her up. Follow me."

In a way, it was a relief to know that we wouldn't have to go in the trailer. Maybe, I was being unfair to him. Maybe, it was neat as a pin. For some reason, I doubted it.

We followed him to a coffee shop a couple of miles away. It was one of those small family-owned places that used to be all over the place. Now-a-days, they were few and far between. Their potential customers were more apt to visit one of the many franchises that dotted the landscape. I remembered a place that was very similar to this one. When I was young; I mean really young; six or seven years old young, I spent a lot of Saturday mornings going to yard sales with my grandmother and as a reward, she took me to a diner that was owned by a friend of hers. Just thinking of it, reminded me of their delicious homemade hamburgers and pecan pie that even now is making my mouth water. Note to self – find that diner. P.S. on note to self, don't bother; it was replaced with one of those franchises.

Once we were seated at a table, I introduced myself and the others to George. The waitress joined us at the table. It was no surprise to learn that this was George's wife. She looked just as tired and worn out as he did. When she announced that her shift started at six a.m. that morning, we understood why.

We let Laura ask the questions. She was our expert interrogator; well, she was the most experienced anyway. Remember all those doors she knocked on, and the Motor Vehicle Branch and the Land Title's office she visited.

She started by asking him where he was born. When he mentioned the town of Harmony, she asked him what kind of town it was to grow up in. One thing led to another, and before you know it, she had him talking about Nolan High. She asked if he kept in touch with any of his old classmates. He answered no. She asked if he knew the where-about of any of his old class mates. He was going to say no, but his wife interjected, "What about that guy over at the drug plant. I thought you said you knew him and the police chief. Didn't you say you knew the police chief? Just the other day, you were ranting and raving about them making it good while you were still working for minimum wage."

"It wasn't the police chief," George answered. "It was the new head of Crimes against Property, Dan Carruthers. The other guy was Chris Raymond. I knew both of them through my brother Tom. When we were in school, I was the only one with a job. I pumped gas every evening while they hung around the swimming hole. The moment I was finished work, all three of them would be hanging around me like leeches, bumming cigarettes, gas money whatever they needed that night. They always promised to pay me back, but they never did. If I had half the money I gave them, we would be living in that brand new double-wide you have been dreaming about," he said while glancing at his wife.

"Your brother knew them too," asked Laura? "Did you say Tom? Is he the one who died in the fire? I'm so sorry."

"Yeah, it's that Tom," George said. "He knew them alright. They all met at camp one summer. I, of course, didn't get to go to camp. I was working. They went to camp when they were in their early teens. A few years later, they went back as counsellors. Dan and Chris were a bad influence on Tom. They may seem nice and respectable now, but back then they were as crooked as they came. Two summers in a row, dozens of cottages near the camp were broken into. Both years, those three were counsellors. I can't say if it was them, but they always had money to spend. The following year when they went their separate ways, there were no thefts at all. That Raymond guy has been all over. He was in the army for a while, and has had a variety of jobs since. Every now and again, he called Tom and Tom would go running. Who knows what they were up to, but I would bet they were up to no-good. How a guy like that gets a good job beats me? You should see the house he lives in. It's a mansion."

"Don't even talk to me about Carruthers. That useless piece of skin let my brother talk him into arresting me. Tom was broke, and Crime Stoppers was offering rewards for almost anything. Tom went and sprayed a park bench with paint and then phoned the tip line accusing me of doing it. Dan came to arrest me, laughing the whole time. Dan probably got half of the hundred-dollar reward. That's the kind of guy he is." By the time George was finished with his story, he was angry.

It was time for us to get back to the Torino's. I threw a twenty-dollar bill on the table to pay for our drinks. There is no way the drinks cost any more than six dollars, but I hoped the extra money would come in handy for the Crawford's. I did not have the money to spare either, but I really felt sorry for George and his wife.

We beat Terry and Becca Torino home by thirty-five seconds. They were turning into the yard as I was closing the front door.

CHAPTER TWENTY

On the drive from the coffee shop, Tracy replayed a part of the recording she made. Whoever had made the recording equipment she was using made quality stuff. You could hear everything we said. I mean you could hear everything. More than one of us slurped when we drank our milkshakes, and I swear we even heard someone pass gas. We teased Tracy mercilessly about that little indiscretion, but in truth it could have been any one of us.

Scott and I only stayed at the Torino home long enough to say hello to the elder Torino's. I drove to the auto wrecker's so Scott could pick up his car. Before he got out, we had a brief discussion about which was the better car, the Monte Carlo or Firebird. When you are young, and often enough when you are not so young, there is only one way to settle that argument. We found ourselves parked side by side at a traffic light. The light turned green and we were off. Of course, we didn't break any speed limits, wink, wink, nudge, nudge, but the Monte Carlo was the better car. The Firebird ran well, and Scott was a more experienced driver, but the long hours I spent working on the Monte Carlo were in evidence that night. When I beat Scott from a standing start for the third straight time, he admitted defeat, gave me a wave and headed for home.

It was fun to push the car to its limits, but there was a price to pay. My gas gauge was creeping towards empty again. I decided to fill up that night so that I could get a few extra minutes sleep in the morning. While I was at the pump, a police cruiser drove by, saw me, and stopped. I had an escort the rest of the way home. His presence was annoying, but I was smart enough to realize that I would have been in big trouble if he had found me ten minutes sooner.

On Tuesday afternoon, I worked my regular shift at the auto wrecker's. Tracy and Laura were waiting for me out front at quitting time. A few minutes later, Scott drove up. We were going to check out Dan's cottage and knowing what we did about Chris Raymond, we were going to check out his properties as well. Our plans had been made the previous evening. Scott insisted on coming along. Now that Brandon was working the occasional shift, he had some spare time.

Laura brought the map from the Land Title's office. Chris' rural property was closer than the two cottages so we decided to check it first. Laura gave directions and we found ourselves somewhere on the back side of nowhere. A couple miles out of town, we turned off the black-top onto a gravel road. We followed the gravel road for a while and then Laura insisted I turn onto a dirt road. It wasn't a very good road, and with four of us riding in it, the Monte Carlo rode pretty low. It seemed like we traveled for miles – that might have been because we were traveling so slowly – before Laura told me to turn again. This road consisted of two wheel-ruts with a grass ridge in between. Before I turned onto the rutted road, I stopped and asked Scott if he thought we would make it. He shrugged his shoulders but Laura said, "According to the map it's not far. Maybe we can walk."

For three of us walking would be no problem. It was a different story for Scott, and yet he was the first one out of the car. "I need some exercise, let's move it," he said.

Tracy was loaded with her back pack. I offered to carry it, but she pushed me away. "I'm used to it now. If I need help later, I'll ask. Thanks."

Laura was busy with her map, Tracy was adjusting the back pack, trying to get it to fit more comfortably and Scott was already fifty yards down the road, his crutches weren't slowing him down in the least. Everyone was busy doing something, so it was no surprise that I was the first to notice the tire tracks that were plainly visible in the dirt ruts. The tracks were familiar. This was the fourth time that I had seen them. The last two times they appeared someone was trying real hard to hurt me. I began waving at Scott, trying to get his attention. I didn't want to shout, in case someone was within hearing distance. Scott finally looked back. I signalled him to stop where he was and using the zippered lips technique; I indicated he should be quiet.

Tracy noticed what I was looking at. While I moved the car to a spot where it was less noticeable, she began taking pictures. Laura walked to where Scott was waiting and told him what we were doing and why. Once the car was hidden, Tracy and I joined them.

This was rough country. We could hear a river somewhere in the distance. Within sight, there were a number of steep drop-offs. Over the years, there must have been some awfully heavy rains to cause washouts like these. The track we were following made a wide turn around a grove of trees. Before we rounded the corner, I snuck through the trees to see what was on the other side.

There was a clearing with some old run-down buildings. There wasn't a vehicle in sight, so I walked to the road and waved the others on. The buildings were in bad shape. One, looking like it might have been a stable, was just a pile of old lumber. The roof had collapsed on another smaller building. According to Laura, one building, that wasn't as bad as the rest, had been a granary at one time. Beside the granary was a barbecue, not old and rusty as you would expect, but almost new. Behind the granary, someone had put up a bit of a lean-to to provide shelter for a strange-looking toilet. It was a chemical toilet. Scott told us that ones similar to this were used by the armed forces. The door to the granary was locked, but there were a number of gaps where the siding had shrunk. I peeked through a couple of them and saw a mattress with a sleeping bag. In the corner sat a picnic cooler. Near it was a shelf holding a good supply of groceries, including bread, and cereal. The shelf was built by inexperienced hands because it was ready to fall off the wall. Someone was living here.

The four of us went in different directions and began scouting the area. Laura called my name. "Malcolm, you better see this."

She was following an old path through the long grass. It appeared as though a vehicle had gone through the grass. The trail ended at an embankment. I crawled up to the edge so that I would not go for a tumble if the bank gave way. It was probably a good thing I did. The edge was crumbling, and it was a long way to the bottom. I peered over the bank and at the bottom noticed the twisted remains of a vehicle. My heart skipped a beat. It looked a lot like my father's old truck. Was this my father's hiding place? Then something else struck me. Was my father lying dead in the wreck down there?

I was going to climb down that hill and find out. First, I had to find out why Tracy was yelling at us. Laura and I joined her and Scott near the granary. She was busy taking pictures of something on the ground. It was the footprints of someone with a crack across their sole. There were hundreds of prints all over the yard. Now that we knew what to look for, we could even see them on the step to the granary and there were a number of them around the improvised biffy. Things were not making sense. If it was my father who was hiding here, then it must also be my father who was trying to hurt me. I do not think so. It was equally as hard to believe he was dead. I was going to have to check out the truck at the bottom of the hill.

The others didn't want me to go. There was still lot of daylight up where we were, but the bottom of the gully was in shadow. "I have to go now," I insisted. "Maybe someone is hurt down there. This might be the only time I have the place to myself. Tomorrow, whoever it is that is chasing me might be back. The three of you can wait in the car. I'll try not to take too long."

They refused to wait in the car. They insisted on hanging around, in case I needed help. I made them agree to keep hidden, in case someone drove up. Remember those night vision goggles that Tracy carried in her back pack, I wound up wearing them. It was almost like daylight. I also had Tracy's camera complete with flash.

I found a way to the bottom of the cliff that was a little less steep than the truck's path. It still took me a good fifteen minutes to make the descent. I didn't look up until I reached the bottom. I was sorry I looked even then. It was going to be a hard climb back up.

It was all but dark when I approached the smashed up truck. I didn't run up to it. I approached with care, calling out as I neared. Was I strong and brave? No, I was scared spit-less. I need not have been. There was no one there. No injured people, no bodies, no one. It was just a wreck.

It was my father's truck. I took dozens of pictures. Thanks to Tracy's expensive camera, I was able to get a picture of the license plate and the serial number. I found the jacket my father usually wore inside the crumpled up cab. I remembered my father telling me about a cubby hole underneath the dash where he kept a couple of twenty dollar bills, in case of an emergency. Without the goggles, I never would have found it, but with them, it was no problem. I found the money, sixty dollars in all. A few minutes ago, I was relieved to know that my father wasn't dead.

Now those fears returned. If dad was on the run, he would have taken his jacket and the money.

It was a tough scramble back up the hill. By the time, I reached the top I was totally out of breath, but the sixty dollars I found was in my pocket and my father's jacket was tied around my waist. The others must have heard me coming because they were waiting for me when I managed with a Herculean effort to haul my bulk onto level ground. They had dozens of questions that I would not be able to answer until I caught my breath.

I was untying the jacket when I heard paper rustling. I checked the pockets, even the one inside and found nothing. I flipped the jacket onto my shoulder and heard the rustle of paper again. I made another more careful search, and this time I found a hole in one of the pockets. I dug around inside the lining and found an envelope.

By now it was pitch dark, too dark to read. I was able to breathe without panting, so I led the way back to the road and the Monte Carlo. While we walked, I told the others what I saw at the bottom of the hill and expressed my concerns about my father's well-being. I was out of breath again by the time we reached the car. I glanced at Scott and saw him wincing with almost every step. By comparison, Tracy looked like she was ready to run a marathon even though she was carrying her back pack that once more contained the camera and night vision goggles.

I was so engrossed with getting in the car so I could sit down, that I forgot about the envelope. We talked about my situation all the way into town. The only conclusion that we came to, was that we needed help. We went to Tracy's to see if her parents were home. Gladys and Steve welcomed us inside. While Tracy waited for that day's pictures to download, she went to her room and returned with a box that contained all of the evidence she collected so far. Gladys made a phone call and when she returned she told us that Laura's parents, Becca and Terry were coming over just as soon as they finished at the theatre.

Once every one was present, Tracy held up the items she collected and Laura explained what they were and where they were found. They made a good team and they must have been convincing because within a few minutes, we were all piling into vehicles and heading for the police station even though it was nearing midnight.

I was the last one to go inside. Dan Carruthers' old partner was on duty at the desk again. He greeted the Torino's politely, but when he saw me his mood changed dramatically. When the Torino's told him why we were there and asked for a senior investigator, his mood grew downright hostile.

"Did you know that kid is a Webb? The Webb's are responsible for about half the crime in this town. You can't believe a word he tells you," he sputtered.

It was Terry Torino's turn to get angry. "You do not know this boy. You have never said a civilized word to him. You would not know if he was telling the truth or not, because you've never let a word he said penetrate your thick skull. Now get me the senior investigator, or I'll have every politician in town, including the mayor, breathing down your neck."

I was stunned at his outburst. It was a side of him I had not seen before. The shocked expressions on his wife and Laura's faces, told me that those who knew him well, were equally surprised. The outburst worked. An investigator, Keith Jones, was called and we were invited to sit down in a waiting area until he arrived.

The investigator told me to enter an interrogation room. It was Steve Torino who told him that we were not going to be separated. He was going to have to talk to all of us. The policeman wasn't happy, but he found a room big enough for everyone and then sent Dan's pal looking for extra chairs.

CHAPTER TWENTY-ONE

For the second time that evening, Laura and Tracy put on their demonstration. This time, they just used pictures. The tire track and foot print impressions were safely locked up in Steve Torino's home safe. We decided that they would be our ace in the hole, brought out if the police refused to take us seriously.

Once they were finished, I told Keith that I was afraid that my father had been hurt or heaven forbid, killed. To say that he was sceptical was an understatement. He excused himself and just as we were about to give him up for lost, he returned. "I have sent a couple of the guys out to the property you told me about. I can't do much else until I hear from them," he reported.

His next words were for the benefit of the Torino's, "I'm not sure what Webb here is up to, but you might want to take everything he told you with a grain of salt. He is probably trying to protect his father. If it is his father's truck, he was the only one who knew where it was. Think about that. By insisting we investigate an executive with the town's major employer, and a well-respected police officer, he is sending us on a wild goose chase in the hope that it will give his father time to make good his escape. Two months from now, the two of them will be sitting at a Mexican Resort laughing at our gullibility. It is late.

You all have work tomorrow and I'm sure these young ladies have school. Take them home and forget all about tonight. Leave the police work to us."

Terry Torino took the floor. "In other circumstances," he said, "we might believe what you say, but we know Malcolm and we know he is not lying when he says he does not know what happened to his father. Even if we thought Malcolm was less than truthful, what does that say about our daughters? They were with him when two attempts were made to hurt him. Are they lying as well? Yes, it is late and it is time we went home, but we are not leaving until you assure us that you are doing everything you can to get to the bottom of this mess."

Keith left the room for the second time. This time he was gone for only a moment. He didn't have good news for me when he returned. He looked at Scott and the Torino's. "Please go home. There is nothing you can do here. We are going to hold Malcolm until we learn more. I know! I know! You aren't leaving without him. Well, yes you are. Malcolm is allowed to have a family member and only a family member with him. The last time I checked, none of you are family."

Becca Torino was livid. "You have his father on the run and his mother is in another part of the country. That is nothing but a bullying tactic, and you won't get away with it. Besides, you cannot hold him here without charging him with something. What are charging him with?"

Keith replied, "I can charge him with obstructing justice, aiding and abetting or even causing a disturbance. I will come up with something, if you don't leave and let me get on with my work. I might even decide to charge the girls over there."

I appreciated Becca's concern, but it was time this whole charade came to an end. I said, "Let me give Uncle Sid a call. He can wait here with me and if necessary he can call my lawyer for me. I'll talk to all of you tomorrow. I will be fine, I promise. Thank you all for everything you have done."

It made a certain amount of sense, but Becca wasn't quite ready to give in. "I am going to phone his mother and let her know what is happening. Tomorrow morning, I will have all the documentation I need to get him out of here, even if I have to adopt him." I was surprised at her vehemence, but I was the only one. Becca was well known for her protective instincts.

I was allowed to call Uncle Sid. I was somewhat surprised to find him at home, and even more surprised to find him sober. That is, I was surprised until he told me it was two in the morning and he had been in bed for three hours.

Even so, my friends refused to leave until he arrived. We were all sitting on the front steps of the building. Keith Jones was not happy about me being outside, but he now knew better than to anger the Torino's so he left us alone.

When Keith was out of earshot, Scott spoke out. "I know a couple of guys working at the drug company. I am going to ask them to nose around out there and see if anything out of the ordinary is going on. I am also calling my neighbour. You know the one I mean, Malcolm. I introduced you the other day; the reporter."

It was good to have friends, and despite the circumstances, we managed to share a laugh when my uncle arrived a few minutes later. Uncle Sid had been in this building a lot of times. Too many times, in fact, but never before did he walk through the front doors. He drove around the block twice trying to figure out where he was supposed to park. Once he found a parking spot, it was time to enter. It was not an easy thing for him to do. Police stations were definitely not his most favourite places to be. He took a few steps towards the building, stopped, looked around and took a few more steps. "Do you think he'll make it, or will I have to get handcuffs and bring him in through the prisoner door, I joked to the others?" It was good to be able to laugh during difficult times.

Uncle Sid eventually managed to overcome his distaste for police and police stations and joined us on the step. I urged the others to go home and get what sleep they could. They left, but not before the ladies gave me pecks on the cheek and the men gave me firm hand shakes.

The second they walked away, Keith Jones opened the door and ordered me inside. I headed towards the semi-comfortable room that we had occupied earlier. The policeman grabbed my arm. "Not this time," he said and he led me to an interrogation room. He didn't join us inside, but he did make sure the door locked when he left.

Believe it or not, for the first time since arriving, my uncle appeared to be comfortable. This was his element and he felt much more at home. He pointed to the camera, microphone and one way glass and warned me that we were being recorded, if not watched. I told him everything that happened that day anyway. I had nothing to hide. It was the same story that we told Keith earlier that night. Once I was finished, there was not anything to do but wait. We sat in the chairs that were designed to break the spirits of the toughest criminals and tried to sleep. There was no doubt in my mind that we were being watched, because the moment I started to nod off someone outside would cause a disturbance. I was awakened by loud laughter, chairs falling and thumps on the wall. Uncle Sid slept through it all.

It was about six in the morning when Keith opened the door again. He was joined by one other cop. He told us his partner's name, but I was so tired that I did not catch it. "Five officers have spent the last four hours at the Mason property. We found the truck that you were talking about and we found a number of tracks and finger prints in the area. Contrary to what you told us, no one has stayed there for quite some time. We talked to Mr. Raymond this morning. He didn't appreciate having to get out of bed because of some punk kid's accusations. By the way, I did give him your name. He has the right to know who is trying to ruin his reputation. I do not advise you to try applying for a job at the pharmaceutical company anytime soon. Now where was I? Oh yes, he told us that he had not visited the property in months. As far as he knows, no one is using the place. He certainly did not give anyone permission to use it. We are checking for finger prints now." He looked in my direction, "You will have to be finger printed. You say you were climbing in the truck and snooping around the building. If you messed up the scene, you will be charged with obstruction. As near as we can tell right now, the only person who has been out there is Blake Webb. I think you already knew that though, didn't you?"

He didn't wait for an answer. He would have waited a long time if had. "Get yourself fingerprinted and get out of here," he told me. "Oh, and do not go far, we are not finished with you yet."

It took them the better part of an hour to fingerprint me. They made me wait until the new shift came in at seven a.m. Once that was finished, Uncle Sid drove me to the Torino's so I could pick up my car. The house looked quiet and peaceful so I wrote a note telling them I would be at home and shoved it under the door.

By the time I walked into the house, it was time to get ready for school. I had been awake for just over twenty-four hours and come to think of it, I had not eaten for about twenty of those hours. Food was going to have to wait and so was school. My bed beckoned.

At one o'clock that afternoon, I was awakened by a ringing phone. It rang several times before I realized what it was. It rang several more times before the cobwebs cleared enough so that I could answer it. It was Scott calling to make sure that I had made it home. I briefly told him about my experiences after his departure. He informed me that he had talked to his friends and they were more than happy to investigate the drug company from the inside. He concluded by telling me that he also spoke to his reporter neighbour. We were not about to get any help from him, or any other reporter, at his newspaper. The day before the staff of the paper was told to lay off the pharmaceutical company. Because the company was a major advertiser, the newspaper's management decided to do just that. In Parkfield anyway, money is more important than freedom of the press. Scott agreed to come by when he was finished work that night.

I was so hungry that I could eat a horse. I was so hungry that my stomach thought my throat was cut. You get the picture. I needed something to eat. A bowl of soup and three sandwiches later – yes, you heard me, I said three sandwiches. I was debating whether or not I should catch my last class in school. The debate did not last long. There would be no school today. I returned to my room to get dressed. I picked up my jeans from the floor where they had landed when I peeled them off earlier. I wanted to see if they were clean enough to wear for one more day. They were filthy, even by my low standards, from my crawling around in the wrecked truck and climbing up the hill. That's when I remembered the envelope that I found in the truck. It was in the back pocket and it was addressed to me, postage stamp and all.

I found a clean pair of pants, put them on and carried the letter to the kitchen. My hands were shaking as I tore the envelope open. A quick glance at the handwriting and I knew it was from my father. The doorbell rang before I got past, "Dear Malcolm". I went to the door and to my surprise and delight; Laura and Tracy were standing there. "Hey, you're not in school. What's up? Come on in."

We went inside and I offered them something to drink. Laura noticed the full coffee pot and decided to try some. I poured a cup for myself and another for Laura. Tracy watched me and slid over another a cup. "I'll have some too," she said. "It cannot be that bad, billions drink it."

I asked again why they were not in school. It was Laura who answered, "Tracy stayed at my house last night and we slept in this morning. Mom and Dad could not complain because they slept in too. We talked them into letting us skip out this afternoon, as well. We told them we were coming over here to check on you. We found your note by the way."

It was Tracy's turn, "We stopped at the store and I told dad what I was up to. He said alright, but he insisted we take these. She handed me a cell phone. She had one for each of us. We are supposed to check with him every hour. They are supposed to be totally secure. No one can listen in, even with the best equipment. Dad is number one, I'm number two, Laura's number three and you're number four. Here's how they work." She spent the next few minutes showing me how it worked.

When she finished, I pointed to the letter that lay open on the table. "What does it say," Laura asked.

"I was just about to read it when you knocked," I replied. I picked up the two-page letter and started reading. I was in school, so my father had written the letter instead of talking to me in person. Things were happening very fast and he had to leave in a hurry. Some very bad people were angry with him because he failed to fulfill a promise. They were making threats towards him and his family, so, in an effort to appease them, he agreed to do a job for them. He would be working with a man by the name of Tom Crawford. He was staying at Tom's for a couple of weeks. He gave the address. I was not to go anywhere near Tom's house, unless there was a dire emergency. I would probably recognize Tom's name, but I might not know that Tom had a less-than-stellar reputation. It was better for me if I went nowhere near him.

So now I knew for sure that my father was in cahoots with Tom Crawford. The police would love to have this letter. It was one more nail in my father's coffin. Not a good choice of words, but that was the image that entered my mind. The letter did nothing to help me figure out where my father was, or who was trying to hurt me.

CHAPTER TWENTY-TWO

Maybe I was too tired to think, but things weren't making sense. I discussed it with Laura and Tracy. My father kills Tom Crawford and torches his house. He goes on the run and finds a place to stay at Chris Raymond's abandoned property. Chris Raymond, the head of security at the firm they are attempting to steal from, knows Tom Crawford and Dan Carruthers. My father destroys his own truck, leaves his jacket and emergency money behind and sets out to hurt or kill me. First, he tried to run me over. Then, he tried to knock me unconscious so I would drown, and finally he tampered with my brakes.

A few minutes ago, my head was full of images of coffins, nails and my father. Was my sub-conscience telling me something? What if the body that had been found was my father's and not Tom Crawford's? That would mean that Tom Crawford was alive and well. Tom might want to hurt me if he thought I was snooping around. Tom might choose to live at his friend Chris' abandoned property. If Tom had killed my father, wouldn't he want to make the truck disappear? If it was Tom I saw running the night of the fire, and he recognized me, wouldn't that give him even more reason to want to get rid of me? This whole scenario made a whole lot more sense than the previous one, and yet there were holes in my theory. How was I to explain the money left on the counter on not one but two occasions? Both occasions were after the body was found. Only my father would leave money. No one else would have reason to. If Tom, Dan and Chris were involved in the plot, what was their motive? It wasn't stealing from the drug company. They were responsible for breaking up that plan. Then there was the big hole. A hole that was big enough to run a train through. The DNA proved that the body in the basement was Tom Crawford's.

These subjects were all raised as we sat there drinking coffee. An hour came and went, so Tracy used her new cell phone to check in with her father. We tried to fit the theft of tires into the puzzle. I told the girls about my telephone conversation with Scott. None of us could figure out why the pharmaceutical company would want to muzzle the press. We kept talking and another hour passed. Laura took out her phone and pressed one. True to his word, Steve Torino answered immediately. Laura assured him we were all safe and sound.

The conversation continued. Laura said, "Let's assume that they killed your father." She took my hand and squeezed tightly as she said this. "They were up to something and your dad interfered. Who took the DNA sample to the Lab for testing? The police, right. Dan is a cop. He might have delivered the sample, or had one of his cronies deliver it for him. He could have switched the sample."

"Didn't you say that your father's key chain was missing from the truck? If it was one of our three suspects who pushed the truck down the hill, they might have the keys. Was there a house key on the ring," she asked as she looked my way?

I nodded yes, and she continued. "It could have been them coming in and leaving the money while you were gone. We know Dan was in the neighbourhood several times. We saw him, both in the police cruiser and in his own blue truck. It might have been a ploy to throw you off track and it worked. It certainly made you think your father was still around. It probably didn't cost them a cent. They most likely used your father's money. They would have his wallet and bank card. Think about it for a second. If it was your father coming into the house, why did he risk coming in early in the day? It would have been a lot safer for him to arrive in the middle of the night. Despite the hour he could have said hello to you.

Tracy said, "She may be right. If they are smart enough to go to that extent to throw us off track, why wouldn't they set up a fake scheme to steal a truck load of drugs so that everyone was looking in one direction while they were stealing from another."

"If that's the case, maybe Scott's friends will learn something," I replied. "Or maybe, we put them in danger. I hope not, but if we are right about these guys, we know they play for keeps. I'm going to tell Scott to have them either stop what they're doing, or be very, very careful. It will have to wait until he's finished work though. He has no phone in his kiosk and if he has a cell phone, I don't know the number. What can we do in the meantime to prove we are right?

That's when I glanced at the clock on the microwave and realized I was going to be late for work if I didn't get a move on. Then I thought, what the hay, I've blown off all my other obligations that day, what's one more? You know what they say, the first sin is the hardest to commit. I called the auto wrecker's and they informed me that they could, indeed, get along without me for one day. It was quiet. It was my uncle who answered the phone and for some reason, before he hung up he told me to be careful.

The coffee pot was empty, it had been for a while, but I picked it up and swirled it around anyway. Maybe I was hoping some of the magic elixir would appear out of thin air. I don't know. I gathered the makings for another pot. Before I could pour the water, Tracy reminded us that we still had two of Tom's neighbour's to talk to about the man I saw running away. It was near-by and it wouldn't take long so why not give it a try.

We took the time to make one more check-in call to Steve. My phone worked as well as the others. I told him where we were going and why. His last words were "be careful". Did these people know something I didn't?

The first house we approached was empty and the new For Sale signs prominently displayed in the yard indicated to us that this house was probably a dead end. We had better luck at the second house. Laura noticed a man, presumably the owner, working in the yard. Tracy and I stayed out of sight while Laura approached him with a recording device that Tracy insisted she take along.

Ten minutes later, Laura rejoined us. Before she said a word, she took my hand and gave me a hug that in one sense seemed to last an eternity and in another was over far too quickly. "I am so sorry," she said! "If what this man told me is true, Tom Crawford is still alive."

I knew what she was getting at. If Tom was alive, then my father was more than likely dead. It is easy to sit at a table and speculate about "what ifs" that you only half believe. It is a different story all together to be faced with the grim reality that a loved one is dead. I have to be honest. I shed tears. Not a few tears, lots of them. We walked back to the house. Laura had her arm around my waist and Tracy was holding my other hand. That is how Scott found us when he drove around the corner in the Firebird.

The four of us were sitting in my back yard when Laura told us what she just heard. James Dornian was the name of the man she talked to. We weren't able to reach him sooner because he was on vacation. As a matter of fact, he told Laura, he left on the night of the fire. Sure, he saw Tom that day. He noticed him hurrying down the back alley. He got into a blue Dodge truck parked right over there. He pointed to the spot where Tracy took the tire impressions. He knew for sure that it was a Dodge because his boss drove one too, a different color of course. When Laura asked him what time he saw Tom, James had to think for a few seconds. He was doing some last minute packing. He remembered because he was in a hurry. A cab was coming to pick him up at eight o'clock to take him to the airport. He noticed Tom sometime between seven-twenty and seven - thirty p.m. He was sure it wasn't sooner. It couldn't have been, because he didn't arrive home until seven and he made a bite to eat before starting his packing. Laura asked him if he was aware of the fire when he left. He said no. He heard about it on the news the next day. It didn't start until after he left. It is too bad about Tom. If he had only stayed out for a couple more hours he might be alive today. Laura asked if he was sure of the time. Positive, she was told. The cab picked me up at eight. I had to be at the airport by nine. My plane left at eleven and these days you have to be at the airport two hours before your flight. I was there with just a few minutes to spare. Laura told him that the fire call came in at seven-thirty. James said that it was possible that he didn't notice the uproar down the street when he left. He was in a hurry and he had things on his mind. It was his first vacation in years and he was meeting a new girl-friend. He was preoccupied. Yes, it was definitely possible that he missed the commotion. Then it hit him. If the fire was burning at seven-thirty and Tom died in the fire, how did he see him in the alley at much the same time? When Laura left him he was trying to decide who to report his unsettling news to.

We listened to the recording Laura made. She had the story right. We knew she did, but we felt it was necessary to confirm something this disturbing. The big question: what do we do now? If you're Malcolm Webb, you eat. I eat when I'm happy. I eat when I'm sad. I can eat anytime, and my stomach still hadn't forgiven me for forgetting about it for nearly twenty-four hours. We ordered a pizza. We were walking inside when Tracy's cell phone rang. We knew who was calling. We forgot to make the hourly call. It was indeed Steve Torino. Maybe Tracy should have told him about James Dornian, but she didn't. She did tell him about the pizza we ordered and promised we wouldn't forget to check in again.

Scott made a pre-arranged call to one of his friends working at Parkfield Pharmaceuticals. The first words out of his friend, Dave's mouth, were, "Where did you hear something was amiss at the plant? Larry and I have been watching and listening and there is something in the wind. Security is nowhere to be found in the plant itself. They are all busy watching the shipping department." Scott told him about our safety concerns and suggested they might want to curtail their activities. "We'll be careful, but we won't stop digging," Dave told Scott.

When Scott was finished with his call, he cleared his throat. "This maybe isn't the best time to talk about this, but what about the body that was found in the basement. Where is it? Is it still at the morgue? Do you remember the city and Tom's brother were arguing about who was responsible for burying it? Lord knows, I spent enough time in the hospital with this foot. I know a number of the doctors. I could call one of them and if the body is in the morgue, they might be able to get another DNA sample for testing. We can find something of your father's in the house, here, to compare it to." He looked in my direction.

Of course, it was a good idea, but at that moment words failed me. I nodded in the direction of the phone and when Scott asked for a phone book, I went to the other room to get it. I took the opportunity to wipe the fresh tears from my eyes. Scott made his call. Whoever it was he talked to, asked him to bring me to the hospital to sign papers. They told Scott to find a comb or toothbrush that belonged to my father and bring it with us. As soon as we finished our pizza, we jumped into the Monte Carlo and I drove to the hospital.

When we arrived at the hospital, the receptionist paged Scott's former doctor. The doctor met us in one of the waiting

rooms. He told me that the body in question was still at the morgue in the hospital's basement. As a favour to Scott, he would take a DNA sample but there would be a fee to have the actual test completed. I gulped. "How much of a fee," I asked?
"Two hundred and fifty dollars," he told me.

It was a lot of money, but it wasn't impossible. I had enough in my checking account to cover it. I signed the papers that he put in front of me and I handed over my bank card and my father's toothbrush. I didn't tell him, I wasn't eighteen. I don't know if that made any difference, but I wanted to get the process started. I didn't want to wait for a parent or guardian's signature.

It was a sober bunch who walked back to the parking lot. The tests were expected to take at least three days, more than likely, they would take five days. Early next week, I would know for sure if my father was dead. It would be nice to know for sure, but in my heart, I already knew he was gone.

I wasn't ready to go home, so I suggested we take a drive past Dan Carruthers' house. It was time for Tracy to check in once more. She did and then told her father where we were heading. "Call if you need any help," he said.

There were no lights on in the Carruthers' house and no vehicles in the yard. We decided to drive by Chris Raymond's while we were out and about.

That's when things got exciting. We drove by Chris' house and noticed Dan's new SUV out front. We circled the block and saw two men, Dan and Chris getting into the SUV. We followed them.

CHAPTER TWENTY-THREE

We had a small problem. It wasn't quite dark and Dan at least, was sure to recognize the Monte Carlo. We had to keep our distance. It wasn't hard to keep three or four vehicles between us while we were in town, but if I guessed right these gentlemen, using the term lightly, were heading for the country. When we reached the outskirts of the city, I offered to stop and let my passengers out. Like that was going to happen.

Somebody's phone rang. We had forgotten all about the phone again. How could we have forgotten? Right now, they were the only weapon we had. Tracy answered the call. This time she asked for her father's help. She told him who we were following and gave our approximate location. He promised he was on his way to pick up Terry. They would be right behind us. "Stay on the phone," he insisted. "Except you, Malcolm," I heard him shout. "You're driving. Keep your eyes on the road."

While he was telling me to stay off the phone, he was busy talking and driving, or so I thought. Do as I say, not as I do. Once a father always a father, I guess. "We're headed in the general direction of Dan's cottage," I said. I looked towards Laura, "Do you remember the directions?"

"No," she answered, and I don't have the paper I wrote them down on, either. It's on my desk at home."

Tracy relayed the message to her father. "Terry is at the theatre. I am picking him up there. We are not taking the time to stop and pick up directions. You will have to tell us where you are. Pay attention to the turns and the odometer. Laura, use your phone and call this number." He rattled off a ten digit number. "Ask for David and tell him to connect your number to the tracking device. He'll know what to do. Malcolm, drive safe. Take care of those girls. Scott! Here's another number. Use Malcolm's phone to call it and ask whoever answers to set up the recorder, then put the phone down your pants or some out of the way place and don't turn it off."

We were well out of the city when the signal light on the vehicle in front of us came on. "Turning off," I shouted. "It looks like they're not going to the cottage after all."

We were trying to stay out of their sight without losing them. We gave them a head start down the gravel road and then we turned off our lights and followed slowly. Tracy took pictures of their tire tracks in case they turned off and we missed it. We were still in touch with Steve. He picked up Terry and they were on their way to help us.

We almost lost them. They turned off the main road and were disappearing over a hill when Scott spotted their lights. Our followers were told of the change in direction. It was completely dark, but things appeared familiar. We were on this road yesterday. We were coming from the opposite direction but it was definitely the same road. The SUV disappeared. It turned off someplace but where? There were no crossroads. I spotted what was more than likely an interior light in a field a few hundred yards away. If I had known they were opening and closing their door to draw attention to themselves, I never would have parked and locked the Monte Carlo so we could continue on foot.

It took us a while to cover the several hundred yards that separated us from the light in the pasture. I was crawling on my belly trying to sneak up to the vehicle when the entire area was lit up. The words, "don't move" were followed by the sound of a rifle being cocked. No, I had never heard a rifle being cocked before, but I knew that is what it was because I could see the bolt being pulled back on the rifle. It was right in front of me, in the hands of Dan Carruthers, Parkfield Police Department's recently appointed head of Crimes against Property. At that particular moment, he neither looked nor sounded like a policeman.

The lights were coming from Dan's blue Dodge truck. Tom Crawford was standing beside it. He too held a rifle. Chris Raymond was leaning against the SUV. "There are four of them. You said it was just the kid. Surely, you're not going to kill them all." Chris might have been a killer but he wasn't a face to face killer.

He was in a real state of panic. I know how he felt. I was panicking a bit myself. I was, after all, one of the four who was going to be killed.

Dan told Chris to shut up and then he walked over and grabbed the phones that Tracy and Laura were holding. He turned the phones off, threw them in Chris's direction and said, "Take these phones and their car and hide them well. Leave the phones in the car in case they have locating devices in them. One of us will pick you up when we're finished with these kids." Dan pointed the gun in my direction. "Give him the keys." I guess I wasn't moving fast enough for him because he walked over and jabbed me in the stomach with the rifle barrel. I sped up, believe me, I hurried.

Chris headed towards my car that was still parked on the road. The rest of us were herded towards a grove of trees. Tom disappeared for a moment and a generator fired up. Shortly after that, a light came on in what appeared to be a large tree house. There was a ladder that led up to it. Tom climbed up first and kept his gun on us as we climbed up. To say Scott had difficulty climbing the ladder would be an understatement. His crutches were useless so he had to hop from one rung to the next. It was a dangerous thing to do at the best of times, but even more so when you had two guns pointed at you. Once he was inside I passed his crutches up to him. It was crowded with the six of us inside. There were only two chairs and you can bet they weren't offered to us. Instead, we were pushed into the only corner that wasn't cluttered up.

"Stay there," said Dan. "He pointed the gun at me and then Scott. "If either of you try anything, I shoot the little one first," he indicated Tracy. "Tom, why don't you back the truck up to the bottom of the tree? There's a hose in the back. You've done a good job sealing all the cracks in here. If we run the hose from the truck's exhaust to that hole," he pointed to large knothole that Tom wasn't finished plugging, "in an hour we won't have to worry about Webb and his friends."

While Tom was preparing to kill us and I was trying to think of a way to escape, Terry and Steve Torino were making a citizen's arrest. They were waiting for Chris Raymond when he arrived at my car. They had no trouble subduing him. Chris wasn't the fighting kind unless the odds were four or five to one in his favour. Neither was Chris the talkative sort. He refused to tell them what was happening to us, even after they found the cell phones in his pocket. The only thing he said was, "You'll be sorry." He repeated it over and over.

Terry used one of the cell phones to call the police. Unfortunately, we were still in the Parkfield Police jurisdiction and it was Keith Jones who took the call. Terry made it abundantly clear that Keith had better get out there quickly and he better have the police chief with him. If they came in with sirens blaring and the young people were hurt as a result, Keith would be lucky if his only punishment was tar and feathers.

While Terry was talking to Keith at the police station, Steve took the other phone and called the number he gave to Scott earlier. He talked for a few seconds and hung up. There was a buzzing sound and Steve pressed a couple of buttons on the phone and suddenly they could hear voices. It was a little muffled, but they could hear me urging Dan Carruthers to talk.

Steve turned to Terry. I am going to listen to this with the ear phones. We are going to have to sneak up on them and I don't want the sound of the phone to give us away. Terry nodded, and after they tied Chris to a fence post and gagged him, they took off across the field.

Back in the tree house, I still didn't know how we were going to get away. Tom was working below us. We heard him backing up the truck and then we heard him rummaging around. Dan was growing restless. "Hurry up down there," he yelled.

"What's the rush," I asked? Then I took a guess. "The theft is taking place tonight isn't it?" I remembered my father's words to Uncle Sid. "Is this the night of the big score; the biggest ever; if all goes according to plan your last one?"

"Your father talked did he? I should have known. Webb's are tough, they told me. Webb's will do anything, if the price is right. Webb's don't talk. Your father was nothing but a bleeding-heart fool. He would steal a load of tires and sell them for peanuts, but when we told him our real plans, he turned on us. He was going to report us. We had him on film, stealing. We threatened to put him in jail for years. Go ahead he says. Put me in jail. I would sooner go to jail than be a part of any plan to mess with drugs at the pharmaceutical company. Sick people might die, he says. Well, guess who died. Your father, that's who, he got in a fight with Tom and Tom hit him with a shovel. He caved in the side of his head. That is what he did."

"Tom didn't know what to do so he called me. I lit the house on fire after I pulled a few hairs from Blake's head. The coroner took a sample from the burned corpse and then I put your father's hair in the evidence bag that was supposed to contain Tom's hair. Just like that Tom was officially dead, and your father was a killer. Tom drove off in my truck that night, but not before you saw him in the alley. He called me to say he saw you."

"The whole charade the night of the fire was to make you look guilty of something, anything really, so that you would be unbelievable. I went into your house twice and left money. It was your father's money, of course. I wouldn't give you a dime of my own. It was Chris' idea. If you thought your father was okay, maybe you wouldn't ask questions. It was also Chris' idea to stage the tire robbery. You want to buy some tires. I have some, I'll sell cheap." He glanced around and chuckled. "Forget I said that, where you're going you won't need tires."

"To get back to your original question, no, the theft isn't going down tonight, but it will be very soon. He yelled out the open door, "You just about finished down there?"

"Two or three more minutes is all I need," replied Tom.

"What about the foiled theft fiasco?" I asked my captor.

"It was more of Chris' games. He wanted an excuse to divert some of his security people from the production lines. My promotion was a bonus. The head of Crimes against Property is in a better position to steer an investigation in the wrong direction than a patrolman. I must admit though, I am enjoying the trappings. It worked just as Chris said it would. Things have been working out for Chris for a long time now."

"How are you going to rip off the drug company," Scott asked him. Scott had sat quietly through the entire ordeal until now.

"Who are you? You look familiar," asked Dan.

"His name is Scott Morgan." I could see one of Tracy's outbursts brewing. "He's a war hero, that's who he is. He has awards and medals like you wouldn't believe. The entire military will be searching for you if one hair on his head is harmed. You don't want that. Have you seen what two angry soldiers can do? They can wreck entire bars. I read it in the paper. Two days ago, two soldiers wrecked a bar. If two soldiers can do that, an entire army will find you and tear you apart, just like they tore apart that bar."

Dan looked in Tracy's direction. The contempt was plain to see. "The army's not going to find me. Smarter people have tried. They won't have a reason to look for me. You see, the army is not going to know soldier boy is dead. They are not going to know any of you are dead. Your bodies will never turn up. Did you see the country around here? We'll drop you in a hole so deep, it'll take you two days to hit bottom." He enjoyed that last bit immensely. He was laughing when he made his way to the door to check on Tom's progress.

I wasn't ready to let him kill us, but I was ready to attack him if only he gave me an opening. I thought I had my chance when he walked to the door, but the gun barrel never wavered. Terry and Steve should have been here by now. They must be lost or in trouble with Chris.

Tom poked his head through the door. "Everything's ready. All I have to do is nail the door shut."

Dan replied, "That's good to hear. Grab some rope and help me tie them up."

Tom came through the door with a roll of rope on his shoulder and a rifle in his free hand.

CHAPTER TWENTY-FOUR

Scott's crutches were on the floor between us. I decided it was now or never. The second I saw Tom's hand reach up to grab the door frame, I lunged off the floor with one of the crutches and jabbed it at Dan. He used the rifle to try and deflect the crutch. At the same time, Laura literally exploded into action. She came out of her corner with feet and elbows flying. Dan didn't have a chance. I wish I could say I did most of the damage with the crutch, but in truth, Laura was the hero. She caught Dan in the jaw with some sort of karate kick and followed it up with an elbow to his solar plexus. Dan stumbled back into Tom and knocked Tom off the ladder.

When the dust settled, Dan was lying on the floor of the tree house, Tracy was holding the rifle and Scott and I each held a crutch ready to hit him if he moved. Laura was standing over him with a foot on his throat. If he moved, she could choke him. I knew by the look in her eyes that she hoped he moved.

The good guys were in control in the tree house, so I chanced a look outside. Tom was on the ground, moaning and groaning with the rifle lying about ten feet away from him. I saw some movement near the front of the truck that was backed up to the tree. Another person was standing behind a tree. I assumed that Chris Raymond was back and by the looks of things, he had help. I asked Tracy to hand me the rifle. I thought I whispered, but in the stillness of the night my voice carried. The person behind the tree spoke.

"Is that you Malcolm?" It was Terry Torino.

"It's me," I replied.

"Is everybody okay up there," he asked?

Steve moved away from the truck. I turned to the others in the tree house. "Are you all okay?" Of course they were; they assured me. This was fun. Tracy went so far as to ask if we could do it again. Maybe I spoke too soon, not all of us were okay. Dan wasn't doing all that well. He tried to mumble something, but Laura applied a little pressure with her shoe and he shut up very quickly.

I pointed to Tom's gun and Steve picked it up. He and Terry carefully approached Tom who was still on the ground moaning and groaning. "My leg," he cried. "I think my leg is broken." He was probably right. Most legs don't have thirty degree bends in them. His did.

Terry and Steve took the rope from Tom's shoulder and tied him up. They were careful to avoid hurting his leg any further, but it didn't keep him from complaining. When they were finished, Terry climbed the ladder with the left over rope. We tied up Dan's arms and legs. I must admit I wasn't all that gentle doing it. We left Dan in the tree house and climbed down. We moved the vehicles so we could light up the entire area.

We were trying to figure out how to get Dan out of the tree house without untying him when no less than four police cars drove up. Keith Jones was there and so was the police chief. Terry told them to call for an ambulance and pointed to Tom. "We have a ghost with a bum leg."

Dan heard the voices and started yelling. "Untie me so that I can arrest these fools. One of my sources told me that Tom Crawford was alive and hiding here. I decided to check the rumour and drove out. I was attacked by these Italian gangsters. They've been in cahoots with Crawford all along."

Until Dan spoke up, the chief didn't know the ghost Terry referred to was Tom Crawford. He looked at him and it would be an understatement to say he was surprised. "Wh...Wh... What's going on here," he stammered.

How do you explain what we just went through? We tried, but with six of us talking at once, seven if you included Dan Carruthers, who wouldn't shut up, we weren't getting our point across. Eventually, the chief had enough and told us all to be quiet. It didn't surprise anyone when he allowed Dan to tell his story first.

I have to give Dan credit, his story was believable. He repeated his earlier words about the informant. He then told his boss who I was and said that I was helping my father, and he indicated Tom, who he pointed out, is obviously alive, cover up a murder. "Arrest them all, the girls, this cripple and the Torino's. They assaulted me, kidnapped me and threatened to kill me. Let me loose so I can call my informant, and try to get to the bottom of this mess."

Steve Torino suddenly remembered Chris Raymond. He asked one of the police officers where he was. The police officer shrugged. "How should I know," he said.

"Didn't you notice him back near the road," Steve asked?

"No, we saw the lights and drove straight in here."

Steve and two officers went back to the road. Chris was still tied to the post, but he had made substantial progress on his knots. Steve told us later, "I don't know what made him the maddest, the fact that we forgot about him, or the fact that we returned before he was able to get the knots loose and escape."

The police still weren't sure which of us were good guys or which the bad ones. They untied Chris, but they locked him in the back seat of the cruiser, just in case. He didn't look happy when they rejoined us near the tree house. I knew how he felt. I was in the same position not long ago.

Dan was still trying to talk his way out of trouble and to a certain degree he was succeeding. The police chief was going to let him go. That would not be good for me, Scott, the Torino's, or people in general. During a moment of silence, I asked Scott for the cell phone I hoped was in his pants somewhere. He handed me one of his crutches while he dug it out. I am sorry to say that I am a little bit clumsy and the crutch slipped from my hand for just a second and hit Dan Carruthers on the shin. If you heard the complaining going on, you'd have thought he had a piranha loose in his underwear.

Scott handed me the phone. I stared at it for a couple of seconds. All I was able to see was a bunch of buttons. I had no idea what they were for. Tracy took the phone from me, pressed a button here and another one there and before you knew it, we could all hear Dan talking, again. This time he was telling a totally different story to the one he told his boss. This time he was telling the truth. Everything he said, every threat; every boast; every incriminating word was recorded on that cell phone. Not a word was said by anybody else. The chief read Dan his rights and clamped a set of cuffs on his wrists. Tom wasn't going anywhere, but his hands were cuffed anyway. Police protocol or something I suppose. Chris Raymond was taken out of the cruiser just long enough for Keith to read him his rights and put on a pair of handcuffs. An ambulance eventually arrived to transport Tom to town and everyone left, but the officer who was assigned to protect the scene until the crime scene investigators arrived.

We found ourselves back in town enjoying Dairy Queen ice cream cones. My feelings were all muddled up. It was nice to know that three very bad guys were going to jail. It was not so nice to know that my father was dead. I wanted to sit here with these people who risked all to help me and yet was it not my responsibility to tell my family what happened?

I came to a decision. I would tell them later. I would get a few hours' sleep and then I would drive to my grandparent's house and with their help, I would notify the rest of the family. I told the Torino's my plans. It was the right thing to do they said. I would not be alone. Laura, Tracy and Scott would accompany me. I would sleep at the Torino's. I wasn't going to be allowed to stay in an empty house. Not today anyway.

I felt a little better knowing that I had a plan of attack. Something still bothered me. I told the others what was on my mind; the plot at Parkfield Pharmaceutical. We didn't know what the plot was, or when it was supposed to happen. We just knew that it was going to be soon. Terry made a point by saying that it was a police problem now. They know everything we do.

"But they don't," I said. "They don't know that the company hired convicted felons."

Steve said, "It is late, although if you want, I know a guy who knows a guy that might get us a meeting with someone in charge out there." I wanted, so Steve reached into his coat pocket and started talking. I thought he was talking to himself until I noticed the ultra-small Bluetooth device in his ear. I was sorry for my bad thoughts earlier in the evening. Fathers do know best.

It was three o'clock in the morning, and instead of going home to bed we were driving to the Parkfield Pharmaceutical plant. Steve found someone who would talk to us. The police already spoke to the company and a vice-president was assigned to check into the situation. This vice-president was already at the plant and because he had no idea where to start searching he agreed to talk to us. The vice-president met us at the gate. "Where's security when you need them," he quipped? "They've all been reassigned, Lord knows where."

"I think that is part of your problem," I told him. "Chris reassigned them so that some of his new hires can operate without interference. We talked to a couple of your employees this afternoon and they told us something strange was happening on the production floor, but they didn't know what. If you check your files to see where the most recent hires are working, you might be able to figure which department is being targeted. I don't know what the hiring policy is, but if any of the new comers have criminal records, or if they were recommended by Chris Raymond, you might want to single them out for closer scrutiny."

"Way to go Malcolm," said Tracy.

"Yes indeed, well done young man," the executive replied. "I'll get to work on the files, if you'll take a seat and wait in case I have a question." Twenty minutes later he was back. "I have found four files that fit your scenario. They are all working on the same production line. It combines the ingredients for a very strong prescription medication and presses them into tablets. The police have been called, and a couple of my senior security people are keeping an eye on the line as we speak. If you would care to join me, there is a place where we can watch while they search the area."

Even though it was four-thirty in the morning, we were in this for the long haul, and we eagerly followed him down a catwalk to a booth that overlooked an assembly line. At a designated time, the line was shut down and two policemen, two security officers, and two men in white jackets entered the room. The police were there to make sure nobody left without permission. The security people began an exhaustive search of the room and the people in the white jackets started taking samples from a number of stations along the line.

An hour later, the white coats were in a lab testing the samples. The security people were locked in a room with two boxes they found in their search and four men were arrested by the police officers. The arrested men were more than willing to talk. Chris Raymond was the real culprit. He gave them the option of co-operating and receiving lucrative paydays, or going to jail on trumped up charges. We all know that any self-respecting criminal will choose the easy money option.

The vice president was jubilant. "You might have saved this company," he said to me. The law suits would have bankrupted us for sure. They were taking the prescription drugs off the line before they were stamped with the name and dosage and replacing them with placebos. The placebos were stamped as though they were the real things, and went to the next line where they were packaged. The real drugs went into large garbage cans designed to store them safely. One of our cleaners was in on the plot. He took the full garbage cans to an empty warehouse. We found dozens of full cans, millions and millions of dollars' worth. The security people found a few boxes of the placebos they were using. The placebos were made right here but on a different line. This company owes you big time. It will be expensive to recall the placebos that have already been shipped, but nowhere near as expensive as the lawsuits or loss of goodwill. If there is anything we can do for you, any of you, just ask."

Steve spoke and the others agreed, "This is Malcolm's show. We wouldn't be here without him. He deserves the credit, all the credit."

I was too tired to protest or to ask for anything. A half an hour later, I was sound asleep in Becca and Terry's spare room.

When I woke up later that day I was a hero, a grieving hero, but a hero none the less. The newspapers had nothing but praise for me. Single handily, I had saved thousands of lives. The people, who bought the prescription drugs illegally on the street, risked overdosing, bad side effects and bad trips. The people who needed the drugs, but received the placebos instead were in just as much danger. The severe pain, that they had to endure because of the fake pills, was only one problem. They too, were at risk of overdosing, bad trips and bad side effects. If they returned to their doctor complaining about the lack of results from their prescription, the doctor's first instinct would be to increase the dosage and frequency. If you believed the papers, I saved them all. I was a hero and Dan Carruthers, Chris Raymond and Tom Crawford were monsters. They deserved to have the book thrown at them for trying to switch drugs. Nothing was said about the temporarily unidentified body and nothing was said about my father; Not a word to help clear his name. The rest of the day was spent with the Webb's. We laughed, cried and remembered my father. Yes, there were a few bad times in my life. On this day, they were forgotten. This was a day for celebrating; celebrating the life of a man who made a few mistakes but was basically a good human being; a human being who died a way too soon.

CHAPTER TWENTY-FIVE

Things returned to normal in Parkfield. We buried my father one bright and sunny day. The DNA samples were retested and proved conclusively the body was my father's. The hospital refunded the money I paid them. The city picked up the tab for the retest and well they should have. I convinced the drug company that he died trying to protect their interests and they put up a plaque in his honor. In addition to the plaque, they gave me a reward. Not a big reward but combined with my dad's life insurance policy, I was comfortable. The house was paid for. My uncle continued to live with me and help out with the bills. My mother allowed me to stay in Parkfield. I guess my actions proved that I was capable of taking care of myself. I kept working at the auto wrecker's. I even attended a couple sales where my boss bought two cars at my suggestion and didn't buy another because I advised against it, Sweet!

I stayed in school. Everyone needed an education, right? The basketball team thrived under its new captain; a junior that everyone liked and whose teammates would, and did, go to the wall for. The football team didn't miss their quarterback. They weren't all that good to begin with, so no one was surprised when they lost the rest of their games. Tracy loved working with the video equipment. She made a documentary that won awards and accolades from one end of the country to the other. She and her grandfather made Scott a shoe-size attachment that he could thread into the bottom of his crutch. From then on, when Scott bought shoes, he needed both.

Joe Grosjean was reassigned to patrolling my neighbourhood. I talked to him often. He gave me my first speeding ticket. His partner gave me my second. Tom Crawford got a twenty-five year sentence for murder. Dan Carruthers and Chris Raymond each got twenty years for conspiracy to commit murder and other charges. Things didn't go well in prison for Dan Carruthers. Not only was he an ex-cop, but he was a jerk as well. Not a good combination in a penitentiary.

Laura and I still kiss and I still look forward to it. Yes, we're still together. My biggest problem now is keeping my hands to myself while we kiss. On occasion, she lets them stray a little further than is appropriate for young people of strong morals such as ourselves. There will be a time and place.

In order to look good for Laura, I tried to lose some weight. She didn't ask me to lose any weight. Doing something like that was not part of her nature nor would she even hint that I should lose weight. So why did I try? I tried, because I didn't want people to think Laura could do better. I'm still overweight. Maybe, it's because I love food. Maybe, it's because I was doing it for the wrong reasons. Maybe, it's because being treated like a hero gave me the self-confidence to be myself and forget what others thought of my appearance. Who knows why? The fact is; twenty years from now I'll still be trying to lose pounds.

We help out at the theatre once in a while, and drive to her grandparent's farm every chance we get. Laura has a driver's license now, but most of the time she doesn't mind letting me be the wheelman. We make the lengthy drive to the farm, because I have a project on the go out there. I found a beat up old pickup parked in the bush. I dragged it into an empty shed and I am presently in the process of restoring it. It will take me years to finish, but when it's done its going to be awesome.

I asked Laura where she learned the moves that put Dan out of commission in the tree house. "I took martial arts lessons for five years. I have a brown belt," she answered.

I was confused. I asked, "If you know martial arts, why didn't you use it when you were being bothered in the school yard?"

Her reply: "I didn't have to. You were there to protect me."

Talk about an ego boost.

The Webb's are acting like Webb's. They're committing crimes, and on occasion they go to jail. Webb's aren't nice people, excepting my father and me, of course.

On the whole, Parkfield is a nice place to live. Every city has its secrets, Thanks to Scott Morgan, the Torino's and, I guess, to some extent me, Parkfield has one less secret.

CPSIA information can be obtained at www.ICGtesting.com
Printed in the USA
LVOW131706080513

332896LV00001B/66/P

9 781460 208267